THE SMUGGLER'S LEGACY

HARDY BOYS ADVENTURES

#25 *THE SMUGGLER'S LEGACY*

FRANKLIN W. DIXON

ALADDIN New York London Toronto Sydney New Delhi

ALADDIN

An imprint of Simon & Schuster Children's Publishing Division

1230 Avenue of the Americas, New York, New York 10020

First Aladdin paperback edition February 2023

Text copyright © 2023 by Simon and Schuster, Inc.

Cover illustration copyright © 2023 by Kevin Keele

THE HARDY BOYS MYSTERY SERIES, HARDY BOYS ADVENTURES, and related logos are trademarks of Simon & Schuster, Inc.

Also available in an Aladdin hardcover edition.

All rights reserved, including the right of reproduction in whole or in part in any form.

ALADDIN and related logo are registered trademarks of Simon & Schuster, Inc.

For information about special discounts for bulk purchases, please contact Simon & Schuster Special Sales at 1-866-506-1949 or business@simonandschuster.com.

The Simon & Schuster Speakers Bureau can bring authors to your live event. For more information or to book an event contact the Simon & Schuster Speakers Bureau at 1-866-248-3049 or visit our website at www.simonspeakers.com.

Series designed by Karin Paprocki

Cover designed by Alicia Mikles

Interior designed by Mike Rosamilia

The text of this book was set in Adobe Caslon Pro.

Manufactured in the United States of America 0123 OFF

2 4 6 8 10 9 7 5 3 1

Library of Congress Cataloging-in-Publication Data

Names: Dixon, Franklin W., author.

Title: The smuggler's legacy / Franklin W. Dixon.

Description: First Aladdin paperback edition. | New York : Aladdin, 2023. | Series: Hardy boys adventures ; #25 | Audience: Ages 8 to 12. | Summary: "Frank and Joe uncover a century-old mystery buried in a New York City prohibition museum"—Provided by publisher.

Identifiers: LCCN 2022048343 (print) | LCCN 2022048344 (ebook) | ISBN 9781665912457 (pbk) | ISBN 9781665912464 (hc) | ISBN 9781665912471 (ebook)

Subjects: CYAC: Museums—Fiction. | Brothers—Fiction. | Mystery and detective stories. | LCGFT: Detective and mystery fiction. | Novels.

Classification: LCC PZ7.D644 Sm 2023 (print) | LCC PZ7.D644 (ebook) | DDC [Fic]—dc23

LC record available at https://lccn.loc.gov/2022048343

LC ebook record available at https://lccn.loc.gov/2022048344

CONTENTS

THE BIG APPLE 1

JOE

O MATTER WHAT, I AM GETTING A BIG, crispy, gooey slice of New York City pizza on this trip. That is the number one priority, as far as I'm concerned," I told my brother, Frank.

He was sitting across from me on the Amtrak train from Bayport to Manhattan, looking over the itinerary for the Bayport High History Club trip. It was a jam-packed four-day weekend of visiting museums and historical sites around New York City, especially those relating to the Jazz Age and Prohibition. Mr. Lakin, one of our favorite teachers, was running the trip. A while back, we'd helped him get out of a tight spot when he was framed for murder during a historical reenactment. Now—even though we weren't regular members of the History Club—if there were activities going on that also involved a major dose of fun, he made sure to let us know.

"We came all the way to New York and the thing you're most excited about is . . . pizza?" Frank said, looking up from his sheaf of papers. "It can't be that much better than the pizza in Bayport, can it?"

"Believe me," I said, mouth watering as I remembered the last time I was in New York and stopped for a classic dollar slice, "it can."

Frank shook his head but laughed. "Well, the Tenement Museum is on the Lower East Side, so that's kind of near Little Italy, I think. We can probably go for your pizza afterward." He paused. "Now you're making me hungry."

"I'll get snacks!" I said. I'd been itching to get out of my seat and walk around for a while. "Chet, want to come?"

Our friend Chet Morton was sitting across the aisle and I knew he was always up for a snack run. "Oooh, yeah. I could go for some chips." He got up to join.

The train clackety-clacked on the tracks as we made our way to the dining car, grabbing hold of the backs of empty seats as we went by to keep our balance. It was kind of like surfing. Train-surfing.

We couldn't decide on a reasonable amount of munchies, so the two of us went back to our seats with our arms full of chips, pretzels, M&M's, popcorn, fruit snacks, and a few sodas. Frank got up to grab some of my haul from me before the leaning tower of snackage spilled and went rolling all over the train car.

We tore into our loot, occasionally passing bags across the aisle and over seat-backs to our other classmates, and watched telephone poles and trees and suburban neighborhoods pass by outside the windows.

"Well," Frank said, between handfuls of popcorn, "I, for one, am excited about going to the Gilded Top Hat. I heard the entrance is super hidden, like you'd never be able to find it if you didn't know what you were looking for. It's not even explained on the website; you have to call and book a tour and then they send you instructions."

I had to admit, the idea of going through some kind of secret entrance into a covert bar where flappers and gangsters went to party to avoid Prohibition laws did seem exciting. It was a museum now, but at one point, the Gilded Top Hat had been the real thing.

"Mr. Lakin told me we should ask the tour guide about NASCAR," I said, looking over at Chet, since I knew he was a fan.

"NASCAR?" he said, leaning over, just as I thought he would. Frank offered him the bag of chips he was holding and Chet grabbed a handful. "What does a museum about bootlegging have to do with stock car racing?"

I had to admit, it was fun to be the know-it-all for the moment. "Alcohol smugglers had to have cars that were really fast and maneuverable. So they souped up their engines to make them as supercharged as they could to lose anybody who might be chasing them."

"Huh," Chet said appreciatively, before popping some chips into his mouth. "Who knew!"

"The next and final station stop is New York Penn Station. Please gather your personal belongings and prepare to exit. New York Penn Station is next." The announcement came over the crackly loudspeaker, and all around, people started murmuring and shuffling and heaving luggage down from the overhead bins.

Mr. Lakin stood up from where he had been sitting a few rows ahead. "Okay, Bayport High History Club, everyone gather your things and follow me. Penn Station is busy, so let's stay together. We're heading to the downtown C train. Everyone has their MetroCard, right?"

I heard a few scattered yeses from the club members. There were fifteen of us spread across several surrounding rows. Once we'd all pushed our way off the train and up from the platform, we emerged into the wide-open lobby area. The other chaperones, Jane Havrilla, a new student teacher who worked with Mr. Lakin in the history department, and James Milstein, a librarian from the Bayport Public Library, walked on either side of the group, corralling us like one of us might wander off. Ms. Havrilla seemed nervous in the crowd, and her eyes kept darting from student to student; she looked like she was silently counting us. I felt kind of bad for her, looking so stressed.

We all piled into the C train. I grabbed on to a pole near the door. Frank got a seat, but then Charlene Vale got on and he practically jumped up to give it to her. Ever since our trip on the Mayhem Express, an immersive murder mystery theater experience that turned into a very real missing person case, Frank had been totally into her. They'd been talking on the phone and texting constantly and had hung out a bunch of times, just the two of them. I could see why he liked her: as the news blogger for the Bayport High newspaper, she was smart, curious, determined, and always on the hunt for the next big story. She took being a journalist just about as seriously as we took our investigations. And it didn't hurt that she was really cute, too. Still, Frank hadn't actually asked her to be his girlfriend yet. I knew he was working up to it though. He was definitely going to do it. Eventually.

"Thanks," she said, flashing Frank a megawatt smile. He opened his mouth like he was about to say something, then closed it like he'd changed his mind, then just gave a goofy smile back. *Yikes.* It was painful to watch.

Frank managed to start having a conversation with Charlene about touring the National Jazz Museum in Harlem. At the next stop, a couple of guys with guitars got on the train and started singing a Beatles song, and I couldn't eavesdrop anymore. When the band was finished playing, one of them came around with his baseball cap out, and I tossed in the change from my snack trip. He was actually a pretty good singer.

We transferred trains at the bustling West 4th Street station, then got off at Broadway-Lafayette Street, near where we'd be staying.

"All right, everyone, stay together. It's only a short walk. And make sure you look up as we go! A lot of these buildings are historical, and the adornments are the most impressive up high," Mr. Lakin said, raising his voice over the sirens and car horns and the rumbling of the subway underneath our feet.

We got to the hotel, and everyone headed to their rooms to drop off their stuff and get settled. We'd all planned to meet back in the lobby at 3:00 for our first tour. When we got to our room, Frank put his suitcase on the luggage rack, so I opened mine up on the chair near the windows.

He clicked on the TV to a random channel that was playing a *Law & Order* rerun. "Hotel rooms are kind of creepy when they're too silent."

I shrugged. I'd already seen this episode and figured out the culprit in the first five minutes. "I never understand why you unpack in hotels," I said, watching Frank move his folded clothes to the empty drawers under the TV. "We're only here for a few days. You can just grab stuff out of your suitcase."

Frank laughed. "Mom has me trained, I guess. Besides, your stuff always gets really wrinkled."

In the background, the TV channel was airing a campaign commercial for a man who, frankly, looked like a Ken doll. Crisp suit, blond hair, blue eyes, teeth so white they had to be bleached. The candidate was looking right into the camera as he sat on the stoop of a building in what seemed to be a busy neighborhood. He declared, "Our current mayor has raised taxes on small business owners, ignored the needs of the vibrant, hardworking immigrant population of this city, and allowed crime rates to soar."

"Huh, I didn't realize New York City had a mayoral election happening," Frank said.

The Ken-doll candidate continued, "My great-great-grandparents came to America with five dollars and a dream and pulled themselves up by their bootstraps. I understand good, honest—"

The alarm I'd set on my phone went off. "Time to head down to meet up with everyone," I said, clicking the TV off.

In a few minutes, we'd finally get to see the mysterious hidden entrance to the Gilded Top Hat speakeasy.

THE GILDED TOP HAT

2

FRANK

I T ONLY TOOK A FEW MINUTES TO WALK uptown to the East Village from our hotel. Luckily, there was a pretty decent breeze, or we would have been roasting. Charlene had brought a water bottle, which was very smart of her, and had her fancy DSLR camera around her neck, as usual. It was her favorite accessory, besides her little spiral notepad. She was planning on writing a piece for the Bayport newspaper about our trip. Ms. Havrilla was passing around a can of aerosol sunblock that was wafting into my face in a choking cloud. Everywhere you looked, the city was busy. People walked tiny dogs and students carried backpacks, probably headed to NYU classes nearby. The smell of street meat wafted from a food truck and—yep, there it was—the smell of fresh New York pizza. I looked back at

Joe to make sure he wasn't being lured away from the group by it, but he was deep in conversation with Chet.

Finally Mr. Lakin stopped in the middle of a block. It was seemingly for no reason and so abrupt that I almost crashed into him.

"Here we are!" he declared, turning back to us expectantly. I gazed up at the storefront we'd stopped in front of. It said, EAST 2ND STREET DELI AND GROCERY—ATM—NEWSPAPERS—LOTTO.

"Uh, Mr. Lakin," Chet said, "I thought we were going to a museum. This looks like a . . . little grocery store?"

"You'll see," Mr. Lakin said, with an impish look on his face.

A moment later a woman who seemed to be around Mr. Lakin's age came out of the store. She looked bookish but also like she could work for a fashion magazine. Her hair was silvery-gray and cut in an angled bob with blunt bangs. She wore large hexagonal glasses, a neat black dress, and brightly colored chunky bangles that clacked together when she reached up to push her glasses higher on her nose.

"You must be Mr. Lakin," she said, walking up to him and extending a hand, which he shook. "We spoke on the phone."

"Yes, it's great to meet you in person. This is my colleague, Jane Havrilla," he said, motioning to her, "and James Milstein, Bayport librarian extraordinaire. And this is the Bayport High School History Club."

"It's a pleasure," the woman said. "I'm Jennifer Hawking, the curator of the New York City Prohibition Museum, formerly known as the Gilded Top Hat. You might be wondering where it is. As I'm sure you know, producing, importing, selling, and serving alcohol were all illegal in the United States from 1920 to 1933. This didn't stop people from indulging in their vices, nor did it stop the distribution of alcoholic beverages. These things were simply driven underground. Hidden bars known as speakeasies were common, especially right here in New York City. Our museum used to be a popular, functioning speakeasy at this location. But the entrance had to be disguised so that law enforcement wouldn't be able to find and shut down the operation. People only knew about the bar by word of mouth."

I looked over at Joe, who was studying the front of the grocery store. It was hard to believe this had once been a glamorous, secret cocktail joint. The building looked old. It had some worn but ornate decorations on the top, like Mr. Lakin had told us to look for, but otherwise it was ordinary. Nothing special.

"In the 1920s," Ms. Hawking went on, "this space was also a small grocery store, operated by two brothers named Sal and Gino Facchini, who you'll hear more about later. Today the business is owned by Sal's great-great-grandson. We'll have to walk through to get to the entrance of the museum. It's a functioning business we share our space with, so please be respectful."

"Our students always are," Mr. Lakin said proudly.

We followed Ms. Hawking into the grocery store, and she smiled at a man behind the counter who looked to be in his twenties; he nodded at her, barely looking up from the newspaper he was reading. We went down a narrow aisle stocked with nonperishable groceries, paper goods, and cleaning supplies. At the very back, we stopped in front of an old-timey wooden phone booth. This place was so tiny, they would definitely have torn it out to make room for more racks of snacks or another fridge for sodas if it wasn't somehow connected to the museum. It must have been back here for a reason.

The curator took a key ring out of her pocket and selected one, then unlocked the door to the phone booth. It swung open to reveal a narrow space that looked almost how you'd expect: a small bench across from a wall-mounted rotary phone. But on the back wall, there was an amazing stained-glass window depicting a landscape scene with blooming trees in front of a lake at sunset. It was backlit, so the vibrant colors glowed like the sun was really falling over the scenery. I'd honestly never seen anything like it. Charlene, who was standing next to me, gasped.

Ms. Hawking beamed. "This is our Louis Comfort Tiffany window. One of our treasures. Louis was an art nouveau artist and a stained-glass designer who was also the design director for his family's company, Tiffany and Company." I could hear a couple of the girls in the back of the group whispering about jewelry. "The window had been hidden in a large safe in the escape tunnels under the museum for decades before we were able to crack the safe and recover the contents. We've restored the piece and moved it here to mark the entrance to our museum."

Sophie Hobson raised her hand from the back of the group. "But this is a phone booth."

"That's right," the curator said, looking pleased by Sophie's skepticism. "Patrons who wanted to visit the Gilded Top Hat would need to be in the know about the entrance and come back here to the phone booth, then dial the correct phone number. It changed weekly, like a password. Now it's always the same, to keep it simple." She picked up the phone and told the group she was dialing 777-7777. As soon as she entered the seventh number, there was a loud *click* and the back wall of the phone booth swung open like a door into a large inner room. Ms. Hawking stepped through and gestured around her. "Welcome to the speakeasy!"

We all piled through the narrow booth and out into a space that could not be more different from the grocery store. The room was large—somehow it seemed larger than the store we'd just come from. It had no windows, but it was lit with multiple crystal chandeliers and art deco sconces on the walls, the light from which was reflected in massive mirrors hanging behind them. Red velvet booths were lined up along one wall and gilded cocktail tables were scattered across the floor. In the back, a mahogany bar with shelves of glass bottles behind it stretched almost from wall to wall. Throughout the room were artifacts in glass cases, and in the center of the floor was a huge safe with the thick door crumpled where, presumably, it had been busted open. I was overwhelmed, taking it all in. I heard scattered oohs and aahs from the group, and people were starting to stray around the room.

"Now, this is our closest approximation of how the Top Hat would have looked in the 1920s, with the addition of the museum exhibits, naturally. There were no windows, for obvious reasons, and the thick velvet upholstery and curtains you see muffled the sound of the jazz music and the loud conversations that would have been happening in the bar. This is the safe I mentioned," Ms. Hawking said, gesturing to the monster in the middle of the room. "After we found and opened it, we moved it here, into the museum. If you step to your left, you'll see a case containing what we found inside, besides the Tiffany window."

Joe and I were standing at the edge of the group, closer to the case, so we got a front-row view. Inside were stacks of cash, some yellowed documents, two bars of gold, faded cardboard boxes that looked like they held ammunition, and a large gun with a round, flat disk at the bottom.

"Some of you might recognize the weapon from movies about this time period—that is a Thompson submachine gun, more commonly known as a tommy gun. It was something of a signature weapon of Prohibition-era gangsters and organized crime operations, including Al Capone. We found several of them in a small armory in the tunnels beneath the museum. Now, if you'll follow me over here—"

The tour continued, and we saw all kinds of antique bartending equipment, including a silver spoon for preparing absinthe, a type of highly alcoholic spirit, which the curator explained was illegal even before Prohibition and would have been extremely difficult to come by.

"Isn't that what they drink in *Moulin Rouge*?" Sophie asked.

Ms. Hawking didn't look like she knew the film reference. "Well, it certainly would have been drunk *at* the Moulin Rouge." Then she showed us a rusted, dented liquor still that looked like a metal can connected to a barrel with a twisted pipe. She explained how it would have worked. "The proprietors of the Gilded Top Hat likely distilled some of their own spirits while also smuggling in Canadian whiskey."

"Is that why they needed souped-up racing cars?" Chet asked, looking pleased with himself. "For the smuggling?"

"Actually, yes," the curator replied. "Smugglers worked hard to create cars that were as powerful and fast as possible to transport illegal alcohol across borders and from ships to storage facilities. Our modern-day NASCAR racing can trace its roots to Prohibition-era getaway vehicles."

There was chatter among the group, especially from a couple of guys in the back, who were apparently fans of racing and found it hard to believe it started with criminals.

"And now I'm sure this is something you'll all enjoy," Ms. Hawking said. "Beneath our feet, there are miles of tunnels extending all the way to the East River. They were used to covertly transport goods from arriving ships to the speakeasy, as well as for the owners and smugglers to get out of the Top Hat quickly in the event of a raid." The curator walked over to a dark back corner, lifted a curtain to the side and secured it on a hook, then pressed against a paneled section of wall. There was a pop, and it cracked outward. She grabbed the edge and pulled open yet another hidden door. This was my kind of place—full of secrets. "Here's the entrance to the tunnels. And this brings us to a little bit of a mystery."

I looked over at Joe, who was already looking at me. Our signature Hardy family mystery genes were kicking in.

"The Top Hat was an extremely lucrative illegal business until the night of April 8, 1925, when the police received an anonymous tip that there was a speakeasy operating at this location. They surrounded the building, trapped everyone inside, and arrested the accused owners of the Gilded Top Hat: Gino and Sal Facchini. The Facchini brothers owned the building and had apparently been using the grocery store as a front for the speakeasy and smuggling operations. They were both in the building that night, and neither made it out via the tunnels. Which leaves us with the questions: Who called in the tip? And why didn't the Facchinis use the tunnels to escape when the raid began? Did they just not have time to get out? Those are questions we've never been able to answer."

The curator looked openly frustrated by this, as if it was something that wounded her pride every single day. "Anyhow," she said, "the Facchini brothers were convicted of a range of crimes including racketeering, money laundering, bootlegging, and operating an illegal speakeasy. They were each sentenced to twelve years in prison." She paused for a moment, still seemingly ruminating on the unanswered questions in the story. Then, with slightly forced brightness, she said, "Everyone grab a hard hat from the hooks over there, please. We've reinforced the ceiling down in the tunnels and there's nothing to worry about, but safety first!"

Everyone moved to the hard hats, trying them on and swapping them with one another to get ones that fit.

"Weird about the Facchinis not using the tunnels," Joe said as he put on his bright yellow hat.

"Yeah, I don't know if I buy that they just didn't have time. You'd think they would have thought of every scenario, if they were such criminal masterminds," I said, thinking out loud. It seemed like there had to be something else at play. Then again, this mystery was almost a hundred years old, and if the curator had spent her career researching it and hadn't figured it out, even Bayport's top teenage private investigators probably couldn't solve it in four days. Probably.

AN ACCIDENTAL DISCOVERY

3

JOE

THE AIR WAS THICK AND DAMP AS WE descended a spiral metal staircase into the tunnel. The stairs looked old, but someone had adhered panels of grippy sandpaper to each step, so at least they weren't too slippery. Safety first, like the curator said. Even so, it was humid in the tunnel and everything felt a little bit damp. I could hear Sophie behind me, breathing heavily. I turned back to face her and my foot slid a little on the step. Okay, maybe they were a little slippery.

"You okay?" I asked.

"It's tight in here," she said breathlessly.

"I'm sure it gets more open once we're down the stairs," I told her. She nodded but didn't look convinced.

Things felt less unstable when we reached the bottom of the stairs, but not a whole lot more spacious. The tunnel was mostly dirt, with wooden beams holding up the ceiling and wooden planks along the ground. The walls were strung with work lights that extended down as far as the eye could see, until they disappeared into darkness. This place was no joke. I could see multiple tunnels branching off the one we were in—who knew how far they all went?

Sophie was definitely also looking down that tunnel and contemplating being trapped in here forever. I could hear her starting to hyperventilate.

"Hey, Sophie, take a breath. You're going to be fine, I promise," I said, turning to her.

She didn't look fine. "It's too tight in here. The ceiling— the walls—what if it caves in? We'll get trapped. I can't—I need to get out of here. I need to get out!"

"I can assure you, it's very safe," Ms. Hawking said. "The tunnels have been inspected by a structural engineer." As if *that* would help the situation.

Sophie's voice had gotten louder, and Mr. Lakin turned around and made his way back through the group to where we were standing.

"Are you all right, Sophie?" he asked, looking at her with concern.

"Please, I want to go back upstairs!" She looked like she was going to cry.

"I'll take her," Ms. Havrilla volunteered. Truth be told,

she didn't look thrilled about being down here either.

"Okay, that's fine," Mr. Lakin said. "You two go back up to the museum and relax, and we'll be back soon."

"There's water behind the bar if you need it," Ms. Hawking said, on a more helpful note. She looked uncomfortable, and I wondered if she was reluctant to let them hang out in the museum unsupervised. But honestly, did she think the two of them were going to make off with the Tiffany window?

Sophie and Ms. Havrilla climbed up the stairs, and the curator turned back toward the group. "Well, if the rest of you are feeling okay, we'll just continue." She started walking down the tunnel. "These tunnels run all the way from here to the East River, as I said. There are also branches connecting to other buildings in the neighborhood. You'll notice that beneath your feet, there are two sets of parallel grooves worn into the wood. Those are where a modified car, which had an augmented engine and extra cargo space, made repeated trips back and forth from the river, carrying crates of smuggled goods to the storerooms below the speakeasy. Now, if you'll come this way—"

Frank, who had been at the front of the group near Charlene, hung back to walk next to me. "Wonder if the getaway car was here by the door to the speakeasy, or abandoned near some other exit the night of the raid."

I'd been wondering the same thing. "Right. Because if it wasn't parked near the door, that might mean *someone* used the tunnel and car to escape that night after all. Like an accomplice. We should ask the curator. Not that we're investigating or anything."

"It's just intellectual curiosity. Mr. Lakin would approve," Frank noted.

When the group followed Ms. Hawking into a side room off the tunnel, I made my way to the front. "Ms. Hawking, do you have the car from the tunnels here at the museum?" I asked. "Will we get to see it on the tour?"

"Actually, no," she said, regret written all over her face. "When we established the museum and explored the tunnels, much of what was down here appeared intact—the safe, the armory I'm about to show you. But we never recovered the car from the tunnels. It's a shame."

Frank raised his hand and said, "But why do you think that is? Where could it have gone?"

The curator looked slightly irritated by his persistence. "Well, we don't know. It's possible others who were part of the organized crime operation escaped the speakeasy that night through the tunnels and took the car or came back for it later. Or that they were out on a supply run that night. Or that sometime in the past hundred years, a contemporary person or persons discovered the tunnels and stole the vehicle."

"But if an accomplice came back for the car later, why not take the valuables out of the safe while they were at it? Or if the car was used that night, maybe the raid wasn't so sudden that there was no time to escape by the tunnels. In that case, why didn't Sal and Gino get out that way?" I asked. If anyone were to avoid arrest using secret tunnels and an escape vehicle, it seemed most likely the bosses would get the first ticket out.

"Well, I suppose—"

"Boys, I appreciate your curiosity," Mr. Lakin cut in, looking like he was wavering between pride and embarrassment, "but let's allow Ms. Hawking to tell us about this room, okay?"

Frank and I exchanged a look, but I shrugged. "Of course. Sorry."

"It's quite all right," the curator said crisply. She gestured around the room. "This was the small arms storage facility. We found several tommy guns here, as well as explosives and ammunition. We actually had to bring in the NYPD bomb squad to secure the gunpowder and dynamite, to make sure it was safe to remove. These, of course, would have been readily available in the event of a raid or a confrontation with a rival bootlegging operation."

"But there wasn't a gunfight on the night of the raid, even though the smugglers were so heavily armed?" Frank asked. I knew this mood he was in. He couldn't help himself.

"There was not. Sal and Gino didn't resist arrest. I suppose if they'd had time to come down here to arm themselves, they'd have had time to take the cars and escape. That's what I've always thought. The raid was so sudden, neither was possible. The police simply did their job too efficiently."

"It all just seems a bit off, don't you—" I started.

The curator gave an indulgent chuckle. "Perhaps you two have a future in historical research and museum curation. Now, if you'll all follow me . . ." The group moved back into the main tunnel behind the curator.

"Don't you think it all seems really suspicious? They didn't try to escape or fight?" Frank murmured.

"Seriously. Why have all that stuff in the tunnels if you're not going to use it to make a stand when you're about to get arrested?" I said, chewing my lip thoughtfully.

Chet, who was walking in front of us, nearly slipped, and I grabbed him before he totally wiped out.

"Thanks, man. They need a dehumidifier or something down here."

"Please hold on to the railings as you walk," Ms. Hawking said reproachfully. "It does occasionally get a bit slippery."

She took us into another side room, dominated by a large slab of concrete. "This is the plinth where we discovered the safe. Cary Safe Company cabinet safes like this one were fireproof and allegedly impervious to gunfire as well. We had to hire a professional to open it. If you follow me farther along, we can see the garage area where the car would have been kept."

The group squeezed out of the room and followed the curator down the main hallway again. As we got farther into the tunnel, the thick, mildewed smell got more intense and I wrinkled up my nose. It was like when you leave a wet towel in the bathroom for too long and it starts to smell funky.

All of a sudden, behind me, Frank let out a surprised, "Whoa!"

I looked back and it was practically in slow motion: his foot had slipped, like there was a cartoon banana peel on the wet wooden floor, and he was falling toward the dirt wall. I reached out to grab him, but it was too late and his elbow collided with the wall with a *crack*. Yikes. That had to hurt. The sound was weird, though. Not a muffled thud like you'd expect for someone hitting damp dirt. This was something breaking, splintering.

"*Ouch*," Frank muttered from the ground, rubbing his elbow. I offered a hand and helped him up.

We all looked over at the wall and there was a square-shaped hole smashed through it, with cracked pieces of wood jutting from the edges and littering the floor below. Frank's elbow had managed to crash through some kind of hidden panel in the wall.

"Frank, are you okay?" Mr. Lakin asked, cutting through the crowd of chattering students.

"Yeah, I'm fine," Frank said, trying to wipe mud off his leg but really only spreading it around. "But what is that?"

The curator was rushing past the students, murmuring, "Excuse me, excuse me, excuse me," under her breath as she went. When she got to the front of the group, she gaped at the hole in the wall. "Oh my. How have I not seen this before? I've combed these tunnels countless times and I had no idea this was here."

She produced a pair of white gloves from her pocket and started clearing the remaining clods of dirt from where they'd been obscuring the now-broken plywood door of the hidden cubby. Then she pulled away the remnants of the half-rotten wood. Inside, there was a metal lockbox, about the size of a shoebox. She pulled it out, and when she looked back at us, her eyes were lit up like Christmas lights. "My goodness, there could be anything in here! I need to open it immediately!"

She looked down the hallway where we had been headed. "There . . . isn't really anything to see in the rest of the rooms. The garage area is just empty and—"

Mr. Lakin took pity on her. "I think it's all right to end the tour here and head back up to the museum. This is history in action! Perhaps you'll indulge the students and me by allowing us to observe as you remove the contents? After all, Frank assisted in the discovery."

Assisted? Frank *made* the discovery! Well, I guess you could say he fell into it. . . .

"Well, all right," Ms. Hawking said. "As long as the students stand at enough of a distance to allow me to work effectively and to keep the contents of the box safe from contamination."

There was a "whoop" and some excited chatter from the group. Ms. Hawking started back toward the stairs, carrying the box like it was a newborn baby. We all followed her and this time, everyone held on to the railing.

THE HIDDEN DEED

4

FRANK

VERYONE HAD PILED INTO THE BACK room at the museum, which was a stark contrast from the glamorous front area of the Top Hat. The speakeasy was all red velvet and mirrors and gilded surfaces. The curator's office and work space were crisp white, perfectly ordered, as clean and sanitary as a hospital. The light was fluorescent, and after the tunnels and the dim sconces of the museum, we were all blinking and squinting while our eyes adjusted.

I was standing in the corner at a small sink, using some wet paper towels to wipe all the mud off my leg and shorts. Ms. Hawking wouldn't let me stand over by the table with the others until I'd cleaned up. Something about contamination. I rubbed at my elbow, which would definitely be bruised tomorrow. This afternoon had sure taken a turn.

Once I thought I was clean enough for the curator, I headed over to the table. She'd opened the lock easily with a small lockpick kit, which was actually pretty impressive. For all her uptight attitude, I wondered if she'd dabbled in petty breaking and entering as a teenager. She had placed the lockbox on a large metal table with a bright spotlight over it that could have been a dual-purpose police interrogation setup. She had on a fresh pair of spotless white gloves and was lifting things out of the box with care, then laying them on the table and examining them with a huge magnifying glass. Mr. Lakin had to keep prompting her to explain what she was seeing.

Charlene was right up front, snapping picture after picture. That had taken some negotiation, but Ms. Hawking finally agreed it was okay as long as she didn't use a flash. You had to hand it to her: Charlene was completely dedicated to a good story. Once she was onto something, she had laser focus and was not going to take no for an answer.

"Is that fake money?" Chet was saying, pointing at some strange-looking bills the curator was spreading out on the table. There were colorful red and blue numbers and large portraits. It almost looked like Monopoly money.

"I'll have to examine it further, of course, but it looks genuine to me. The graphic design of US currency has changed over the years."

The curator moved the money aside, seemingly tempted by the large stack of curling yellow documents underneath. She separated them slowly, occasionally using some very light steam from a small machine on the edge of the table, or wiggling a piece of acid-free paper between sheets that were stuck together.

"These appear to be receipts and financial records relating to the smuggling operations and profits from the bar," Ms. Hawking was saying, bent over something that looked like a ledger and studying it with her magnifying glass. "We have some others that were found in the larger safe. I'll have to cross-reference them." She sounded like there was nothing she would love to do more.

"How can you even read that?" asked Sophie, who was looking much better after her ordeal in the tunnels. She and Ms. Havrilla had gone into the grocery store and gotten ginger ale, which they had been drinking in one of the plush booths when the rest of the group emerged from the tunnel. The curator looked like a shaken soda can about to explode for a moment when she saw the drinks inside the museum, but ultimately just told them beverages weren't allowed in the back room. I think the two of them were pretty lucky Ms. Hawking was in such a good mood about the lockbox.

"All that writing just looks like random curlicues," Sophie finished.

Ms. Hawking actually half smiled. "It's true, handwriting was quite different back then. You get used to reading it."

There were pages that were solid blocks of handwriting, like journal entries, which the curator laid out side by side on the table. "This handwriting looks like it matches a lot of the other documents we have relating to the running of the speakeasy. I believe it is Sal Facchini's. This will be fascinating to read."

I would seriously not have put it past her to scan the documents and take them home to read after work like most people read a best-selling novel.

At the bottom of the box was a clump of documents that were really stuck together. They were overlapping and creased, and some of the ink was smeared from moisture. Ms. Hawking lifted the bunch out and set to work, very carefully trying to separate the pages. She'd apply a burst of steam, slowly insert a fresh piece of paper between the sheets, then take a piece of white, waxed dental floss and shimmy it between the pages to pry them apart. Eventually, there were six separate pages on the table with what looked like minimal damage.

Mr. Milstein, who had been mostly quiet, broke out in a small round of applause. "Oh, bravo! Excellent work!"

Ms. Hawking flushed. "Oh, well, years of training. What sort of conservator would I be if I couldn't separate sticky pages? But thank you."

Mr. Milstein's wife had left him several years ago. The rumor was that he spent too much time at work and she'd had it. He was a nice guy, though. I wondered if this was his idea of flirting. It was . . . well, an attempt had been made.

The curator was hunched over the documents with her magnifying glass and let out a gasp, practically a squeal. She picked up one of the pieces of paper and held it to the light. It was typeset and looked official. Her eyes darted over it and she whispered, "Oh my. I can't believe—"

"What is it?" Mr. Lakin asked, taking a step closer to the table.

"It looks—it looks like a deed. For the whole building, including the back space where the bar was. But that doesn't make sense; we already have the deed. It's in a case in the front, in the name of Gino Facchini. This one—"

She trailed off and leaned in close with the magnifying glass. "What—this can't be a genuine document."

"What is it?" Mr. Lakin repeated more insistently, excited.

"It's in a different name," she said, not looking up from the document. "But—"

She went over to her desk and picked up a few other old-looking documents inside plastic sleeves. She examined one, then another, then yet another with her magnifying glass.

"Fascinating," she murmured.

"What?!" Chet burst out.

Ms. Hawking looked up, her face mystified, with a tinge of irritation at the edges, in response to Chet's outburst. "This document lists someone named Richard Kensington as the owner of the building, suggesting he may have been the proprietor of the Top Hat. Or perhaps he was renting all the space out to the Facchinis, but at the very least, he was likely in the know about the bootlegging activities happening in his building. The signature . . . The handwriting on all the records we have from the bar is very distinctive in the way the letter *e* connects to other letters. I've seen it so often I would recognize it anywhere. The *en* in Kensington matches it. Whoever signed this deed—I think it's possible he wrote many of the other business documents we have. Unless Richard Kensington is just an alias for one of the Facchinis. . . . This changes everything."

"Are you saying that the Top Hat was actually owned and operated by someone else?" I asked, ideas racing through my mind. There were a lot of small, annoying inconsistencies in the story we'd been told about the night of the raid. Now it seemed like maybe there was more going on after all. "Like maybe the Facchini brothers just worked for them? Or maybe they were just scapegoats and not involved with the speakeasy at all?"

"Now, let's not jump to conclusions," Ms. Hawking said. "Part of being a historian is remembering to focus on facts and research. We have to look at the documents at hand before making a determination. This isn't an episode of one of those true crime shows." Everyone around the table looked kind of bummed, so she added, "But it does cast some doubt on what we thought we knew about the criminal organization behind the Top Hat and who was involved. Apparently it all goes much deeper than we knew."

"This is living history!" Mr. Lakin said appreciatively. "New discoveries are being made all the time that challenge what we thought was fact. It's very exciting. Thank you for sharing this discovery with us, Ms. Hawking."

Technically, I thought, it was my discovery. My elbow throbbed in agreement.

"Well! It's been an exciting afternoon. I hope you enjoyed your visit," Ms. Hawking said, already ushering us toward the door. I was sure she'd be pulling an all-nighter in the back office.

Once we'd filed out through the phone booth, she shut the outer door. Then I heard the inner door click behind that. She was not wasting another second on us. I looked over at Joe, whose eyebrows were raised.

"Sheesh, she's in a hurry," he said.

"Can't blame her, I guess. This must be a massive discovery," I said. "I'd love to know what's in the rest of those documents. Do you think those journal pages were written by that Richard Kensington person?"

Chet and a bunch of the others were gathering up snacks to take back to the hotel for later. I grabbed some barbecue chips and gummy bears and headed up to the front. I put them on the counter, and the cashier was scrolling on his phone. He tore his eyes away from it and rang up the items, plus a bunch of other snacks Joe was dumping next to them too.

"Excuse me," I said, hoping this wasn't out of line. "I was wondering, do you know the family that owns the store?"

The man looked up from the bottle of iced tea he was scanning. "Why?"

"Oh, well, we just came from the museum," I said.

"Yeah, I saw," he replied in a monotone.

"The curator said the store is being run by the same family who ran it in the 1920s, so I just wondered if you knew them. The Facchini family?"

"Sure. They don't want anything to do with what she's told you in there, though. It's awkward enough to have an entire museum dedicated to your family's supposed criminal history. They don't need to be right out here every day for interviews after tours, like part of the exhibit." The cash register dinged. "That's seventeen fifty."

I extracted a crumpled twenty from my pocket. Luckily, it hadn't been saturated with mud. "Oh, I didn't mean to dredge up anything sensitive. When you say, 'supposed,' do you mean the family feels the charges were mistaken?"

The man shrugged. "It was generations ago. Here's your change." He dropped it into my hand and went back to his phone.

The thing was, he seemed like he did care about these things from generations ago. He was chewing on his lip as he stared back down at his phone, looking irritated.

"All right, Bayport historians! We're heading over to John's of 12th Street for an early dinner. It's an Italian restaurant now, but it used to be yet another speakeasy that was a favorite of mobster Lucky Luciano. I don't know about you, but all this history has made me hungry," Mr. Lakin said, leading the group toward the door. I followed Joe out but took another look back at the guy, who was rearranging packs of gum on the counter restlessly.

Outside, Charlene walked up next to me. "What was that about, with the guy in the shop?"

I furrowed my brow. "I don't know. He said he knows the Facchini family and they don't want anything to do with the museum. And he suggested that the family believes the brothers were wrongly convicted. He really didn't seem to want to talk about it, though."

"I mean, if your ancestors went to prison for bootlegging and racketeering and all that and there was a museum right behind your shop that's basically dedicated to it, that's got to be uncomfortable," Joe said.

"But now there's this Richard Kensington," Charlene mused. "Maybe Sal and Gino weren't at the top of the chain after all. I got some good shots here." She was walking down the busy sidewalk while simultaneously looking at the small viewscreen on her digital camera, zooming in on shots of the documents. "I can't wait to download and enhance them on my laptop later."

Charlene was sharp, always questioning things and trying to piece together clues. That's why she was such a good journalist. She'd be a great detective, I thought. I smiled over at her, but she was too absorbed in her camera to notice. I considered asking if I could stop by and look at the photos with her later; I genuinely wanted to see what was in them and also hang out with her. But then I thought maybe it would be better to wait and see if she invited me. Since we'd been hanging out so much lately, it seemed like it all should have been more natural by now, but it was hard not to over-analyze everything.

"That's what I'm thinking. Maybe Kensington was their boss," I said, refocusing on the conversation.

"Or maybe 'Richard Kensington' is just an alias for one of them. Like a fake name to use for official purposes. And the police got it right after all," Joe added.

I mulled over this as we crossed the street and walked down the block, following the group. There were some political campaigners standing on the corner, handing out flyers up ahead. Charlene breezed past them without engaging, like a true New Yorker, but I didn't dodge fast enough.

"Don't forget to vote Trent for mayor!" a peppy young woman said, stuffing a flyer into my hand.

"Uh, I'm not—" I started.

Joe laughed. "Come on, Frank." He tugged my arm through the swarm of over-caffeinated political volunteers, and I shoved the paper into my backpack.

BURIED FOR A REASON

5

JOE

FRANK WAS TAKING WAY TOO LONG getting ready in the hotel bathroom. While I waited, I was nursing my coffee and soggy Froot Loops from the continental breakfast and half watching the news.

"Hey, I know we're supposed to be going to the Metropolitan Museum this morning, but since we've been there before, do you think Mr. Lakin would let us go back to the Prohibition Museum? Maybe we can ask Ms. Hawking to let us work on the documents with her. I just kind of can't stop thinking about everything that happened with the raid and the two deeds. It's bugging me," I said, hoping he could hear me over the bathroom fan.

Frank poked his head out the door with a toothbrush in

his mouth and mumbled around it. "He is always saying that the History Club is about sparking our interest in the past and uncovering the lesser-known events that shaped the future and all that. . . . Well, my interest is sparked! And my elbow was what did the uncovering yesterday, so I feel like it's only right that we get to follow up."

"Exactly!" I said. "And if someone's family has been wrongly called gangsters and crooks for decades, I think that's worth investigating. Chief Olaf isn't even here to disapprove." I gave Frank a little smirk. Chief Olaf was the chief of police in Bayport. We'd solved a few too many cases out from under him, so he wasn't a huge fan of us and our detective work. But that wouldn't be a problem in New York City.

Frank chuckled. "True."

The rest of the club was assembling downstairs. We found Mr. Lakin at the front of the group, sipping an iced coffee and talking to Mr. Milstein. He brightened when he saw us.

"Ah, Hardys! Good morning! Are you looking forward to viewing some art deco masterpieces at the Met?" He'd clearly already had his fair share of caffeine for the morning.

"Uh, actually, we had a question," I said, exchanging a glance with Frank. "We've been to the Met a few times already, so we were hoping we might be able to go back to the Prohibition Museum. We're so interested in the documents that were discovered yesterday and what they'll mean for the history of the speakeasy. It would be great to keep watching that process. If Ms. Hawking will have us. And you don't mind."

Mr. Lakin seemed to consider for a moment, then gave an amused smile. "Actually, someone beat you to it! Charlene asked last night if she could continue following the story at the museum, so I asked Ms. Hawking. It took a little convincing, but she said it was okay. I don't see why you boys can't tag along as well. Ms. Havrilla is going to chaperone; you can join the two of them over there." Mr. Lakin gestured toward the check-in desk, where Charlene was looking through her spiral notepad and Ms. Havrilla was reading something on her phone.

Tag along! Sheesh. Charlene got the jump on us. I looked over at Frank, who seemed totally satisfied with this outcome.

"Well, she's a great investigative journalist! I'm sure she'll be just as on top of figuring all this out as we are. The more, the merrier, right?" he said.

"Sure," I said as we headed over toward Ms. Havrilla and Charlene. "It'll be great."

"Hey, you two. What's up?" Charlene said, looking up from her notes. "Heading to the Met soon?"

"Actually," Frank replied, "we asked Mr. Lakin if we could split up from the group to go back to the Prohibition Museum, and he said someone else already had the same idea."

Charlene smirked teasingly. "You've gotta wake up earlier than this to scoop me, Hardy. This story is bigger than

I expected, by a lot. I'm thinking I might be able to write about the discovery for a major paper. After all, I can give an eyewitness account from the tunnel."

"Do you need a quote about what it was like to fall into the secret compartment?" Frank asked. "Because the experience is still very fresh in my memory."

She laughed. "I'll have to take you up on that."

"Okay, you three. Let's head to the train," Ms. Havrilla said, looking down at the maps app on her phone. The museum wasn't far, and I was pretty sure we'd be fine getting there without looking at directions, but Ms. Havrilla seemed like the kind of person who needed that extra bit of verification. She guided us out of the hotel and we walked for a few blocks; Ms. Havrilla constantly glanced from her phone to the street signs to each of us in turn, as if to make sure we were all still there.

We headed down into the subway station, swiped our cards, and hopped on the train. It was after the morning rush, so while it was crowded, we weren't completely jammed into the car.

"I wonder if the curator has made a transcript of those journal pages yet," Charlene said. "She seemed pretty confident she'd be able to read them without any problems."

"She probably has them memorized by now," I said. "She seemed like she couldn't wait for us to leave yesterday so she could get started."

"I've been thinking about what she said, about the

handwriting," Charlene mused. "She must have so many documents to compare the signature on that deed to, and I know she said she recognizes the lettering. But I wonder if she has handwriting samples that are a hundred percent verified to be from the two Facchini brothers. Like, did she just assume the Gilded Top Hat records she has were written by them, since they were the ones arrested?"

"Maybe we can get that guy from the store to ask his bosses if they have any old family papers," Frank said.

"He didn't seem to want anything to do with us yesterday, though," I reminded him.

"True," Frank conceded. "But maybe if we explain the new information and the fact that this document might prove the bar was owned by Richard Kensington, he'll want to help us."

"It's worth a try, anyway! I can talk to him. I'm good with interviewing sources and asking them for information," Charlene volunteered.

"I don't know why, but I can't shake the feeling that that name is familiar. 'Kensington.' Like I've heard it somewhere recently," Frank said.

"Maybe it was in one of the zillion *Law & Order* episodes we watched last night," I said.

Frank shrugged. "Yeah, maybe."

When we got to the East 2nd Street Deli and Grocery, we headed through the door and saw an unfamiliar boy who looked like he was in his late teens behind the counter. We asked if he knew the owners, and he said he'd only just started working there, and who we really wanted to talk to was Nicky Facchini. He was the boss. But Nicky wasn't there now and the guy didn't know if or when he was coming in for the day. Maybe later in the afternoon. I described the man who had checked us out the day before, and the cashier said he thought that sounded like Nicky, maybe. But it also kind of sounded like another guy who worked there sometimes, who played bad music too loud, according to the kid.

Bummer. That was a dead end for now.

We headed back to the phone booth, which was unlocked today. Charlene went in first, picked up the phone, and referred to her notebook before dialing 777-7777. There was a ringing sound, and then the back of the phone booth clicked and swung open. We all walked through into the museum.

There was a woman standing in the bar area today. She had shoulder-length black hair and was wearing a white lab coat and white gloves.

"Oh! There are four of you. Jennifer only told me to expect two," she said. She seemed nonchalant about it, like it was a fun surprise. I had a feeling the curator might not feel the same way. I guess Mr. Lakin hadn't gotten a chance to call ahead. "I'm Mona, the assistant curator. You can come on back with me."

She locked the outer door of the phone booth, clicked

the inner door with the stained-glass window in it shut, then gestured for us to follow her. Frank and I exchanged a cringey look as we walked back toward the office. Ms. Hawking did not seem like the kind of person who appreciated surprises.

"Jennifer!" Mona said. "The students are here with their teacher."

The curator looked up from her table, which was completely covered with curling, yellowed documents. Some were in plastic sleeves. She was examining one of them with her large, lighted magnifying glass.

"Oh, I see there are . . . more than expected," she said. "It's you two boys. The ones with all the questions."

"Yeah, hi. I'm Joe and this is my brother, Frank. Sorry Mr. Lakin didn't get a chance to call to give you a heads-up. We asked this morning if we could join Charlene. We're really curious about the documents and what you've been able to find out. Your work is so interesting." I put on my most charming smile.

Ms. Hawking paused, then said, "It is interesting, indeed. Well, since you're all here, you can come on over. But you"— she looked toward Charlene—"just remember, no flash photography, please. It would be harmful to the documents."

"Of course. Got it!" Charlene said, pressing a button on her DSLR. She stuck the lens cap in her pocket and we all walked over to the table.

There were stacks and stacks of cash. Ms. Hawking said, "There appears to be fifty thousand dollars here, all genuine, as far as I can tell. Taking inflation into account, that would be approximately seven hundred thousand dollars by today's standards. It's a very significant amount of money. Whoever left it must have been in a huge hurry."

I looked over at Frank, whose brow was scrunched up, thinking. The escape car was gone; the lockbox was left behind. Huh.

"These documents," she continued, "are ledgers that show how money was being laundered through the Facchini grocery store. Do you know what that means, to launder money?"

"Sure!" Charlene said. "Transferring money obtained from crimes through a legitimate business to obscure where it came from. So they were taking proceeds from the speakeasy and the smuggling and making it look like they came from purchases at the grocery store?"

"Yes, precisely. It was a large volume of money, though, to run through a business that wouldn't have been making huge profits. And after examining copious handwriting samples, I'm no longer sure the ledgers were written by Sal. If you look here"—she moved to the other end of the table and pointed to a cluster of pages covered in looping script—"these are the journal pages from the lockbox, which detail things about the day-to-day running of the speakeasy. It's difficult to be sure, since there isn't a lot of handwriting on the deed to match with, but I'd say they very well could have been written by the man who identifies himself as Richard

Kensington. There are also some similarities between the script in the ledgers and the journal."

"So the bookkeeper might have been this 'Richard Kensington,' not one of the Facchinis?" Charlene asked. "Maybe Kensington was their employee or partner. Or the Facchinis weren't even in charge of the money laundering that was going through their own store!"

"That's precisely what I'd like to figure out. I've reached out to a colleague of mine who is a chemist and specializes in analysis of historical ink—"

Ms. Hawking was interrupted by a loud *smash* from outside. Ms. Havrilla let out a shriek, which made Mona jump. The smash had sounded like the time, when Frank and I were younger, that we were playing catch with a baseball in the yard and I accidentally rocketed the ball through our kitchen window.

Oh man. *Window.*

Ms. Hawking was frozen, eyes wide. "What . . . was *that*?" she murmured.

Charlene was the first to turn and run out the door, so we all followed her into the dimly lit front room. The light from the crystal chandeliers was catching and glittering on countless shards of colored glass littered all over the floor at the front of the museum. Somehow, the priceless Louis Comfort Tiffany window had been completely smashed.

The curator ran up to the edge of the sea of glass and started screaming, as if there had been a murder. Mona went up to her and patted her arm in a vaguely comforting way, but she looked seriously disturbed too.

"How . . . how did this happen?" Mona asked no one in particular, voice trembling. "I swear I locked the outer door after they came in, Jennifer. I know I did."

There was something big and rectangular in the middle of the shards of glass. I was wearing my boots, since it was supposed to rain later that day, so I carefully made my way to it, making sure to avoid stepping on any of the shards that were big enough to be salvaged. The object was a brick. Someone had thrown a brick through the window. This had been intentional.

I knelt down and picked up the brick, which had a piece of paper and a rubber band wrapped around it. I pulled the paper out from under the rubber band and held it up so I could read it. In large block letters written with black Sharpie marker, it said, *THE PAST IS BURIED FOR A REASON. STOP DIGGING OR YOU WILL BE STOPPED.*

FRANK

I MADE MY WAY OVER TO WHERE JOE WAS standing, being extra careful since I was only wearing sneakers. He showed me the brick he'd picked up and handed over a crumpled piece of paper. I read it and my adrenaline started pumping. This hundred-year-old cold case wasn't so cold anymore. "Someone knows about the documents."

"Someone who doesn't want people finding out what they say," Joe said, taking back the note.

"What do you mean? What is that?" Mona asked, coming closer and craning her neck to see the note. Joe held it out so the others could see it and explained what we had found.

"I'm going into the store to see if anyone saw anything. You should call the police," I said. Joe nodded. I walked to the phone booth, crunching with every step, and swung open the inner door, which now had a jagged hole in the middle. The outer door was wide open, and it was clear the lock had been tampered with—it looked like it had been pried open.

I hurried through and down the aisle into the grocery store, looking left and right to see if anyone was still there. The place looked pretty empty.

"Hello?" I called. "Is anyone in here?" After I'd been up and down all the aisles and concluded that there weren't any customers, I went up to the front counter. The same man from yesterday was there now. He had earbuds in and was bobbing his head to some music, with a newspaper spread wide before him. How could he seriously just be sitting there? Had he missed the huge crash?

"Hello!" I stepped into his range of sight, and eventually he looked up and saw me. I pointed to my ears, and he pressed the screen of his phone and took the earbuds out.

"Sorry. What can I help you with?" he said.

"You didn't hear anything just now?" I said, honestly in disbelief. "Someone vandalized the museum back there. The Tiffany window got smashed with a brick."

The guy looked shocked and stood up from his stool. "What? Just now?"

"Yeah, just a minute ago. Are you listening to heavy metal or something?"

He shrugged. "I like it loud. Did anyone get hurt? Should I call the cops?"

I looked him in the eyes, trying to decide if his reaction was genuine. It was hard to believe that some vandal had come into his shop with a brick, walked to the back, pried the door open and smashed the window, then likely come running up the aisle and out of the store, all while this guy had been sitting right behind the counter and noticed nothing.

"No, they're already calling the police. They should be here soon." I waited to see if his expression would change, but he didn't show any notable response. "Did you see anyone come in?"

The man considered. "Now that you mention it, some suit did come in a bit ago. I just saw him out of the corner of my eye. Only noticed because we don't get them too often. Those business types aren't really around this area."

"You saw him come in before the window got broken?" I asked.

"Well, I don't really know when it got broken, but it was a little while before you came up to me. Not sure when he left. I wasn't paying attention."

"Can you describe him?"

The guy threw up his hands, like it was an unreasonable question. "I dunno, kid. He was white, brown hair, I think, fancy suit. I was reading the paper. Gimme a break!"

I pointed up to a security camera I saw in the corner of the store. "That footage—is there a camera that captures the door of the phone booth?" I asked. "The police are going to want to see all of it, I'm sure."

"Oh," the guy said, looking slightly sheepish. "Security cams are expensive. Those ones are for show. They don't record anything."

Wow. Total dead end. "Okay, well, thanks. When the officers get here, they might want to talk to you again," I said.

He was already sitting back down on his stool and leaning over his newspaper again. For someone who had just been mere feet from a vandalism incident, he seemed remarkably unbothered. "Sure. I'll be here."

Back inside the museum, Ms. Hawking and Mona were sitting in one of the red velvet booths. Someone had gotten them both glasses of water and Mona was sipping at hers, sniffling. Ms. Havrilla was standing next to her and patting her on the shoulder in a "there, there" sort of motion. Ms. Hawking had the note spread out flat on the table in front of her and was just staring at it, eyes slightly glazed. Charlene was walking around the perimeter of the area that was littered with glass shards, taking crime scene photos.

"I don't understand," Ms. Hawking was saying quietly. "I just don't understand."

"Between the time we left the museum yesterday and now, who all have you talked to? Who else knows about the documents we found besides you two and our group?" Joe was asking her.

"Barely anyone," Ms. Hawking said. "I called Mona—"

"And I didn't tell anyone! Not even my partner!" Mona interjected. "I promise!"

"I know, Mona," Ms. Hawking said. "It's okay. After that, I made scans of some of the documents and put them on my tablet, then took them to consult with a few other experts. I spoke to a colleague at the New-York Historical Society, a research librarian at the New York Public Library, and my friend at the New York City Department of Records. That was it, just Mona and those three. And I didn't give copies of the documents to any of them. They're all people I've worked with for years, who are dedicated to the preservation of history. They would never do this."

"Maybe one of them told someone else about the documents," I suggested. "They could have consulted a colleague about whatever you asked them, maybe. Would that be possible?"

"Well, I'm not sure. Maybe," Ms. Hawking conceded.

"Hello?" came an unfamiliar voice from behind us. We all turned around, and there were two police detectives making their way in through the phone booth. "Is Jennifer Hawking here?"

"Please be careful!" Ms. Hawking exclaimed, knocking the table and sending water sloshing over the rim of her glass in her haste to get up and out of the booth. "That's a priceless Tiffany window, and I don't want any of the pieces that can be salvaged getting broken more than they already are."

"Understood," the first detective said. He was short and broad-shouldered, with a sharp, angular jaw. He carefully made his way to the edge of the patch of broken glass, followed by the other detective. "I'm Detective Eric Santos, NYPD. This is my partner, Detective Emilia Smart."

The female detective behind him, who was tall and imposing, like she definitely went to CrossFit, nodded toward us. "We have a couple of crime scene techs coming in here in a minute. Has anyone touched or moved anything from this area?" She gestured all around them.

I grabbed the brick, rubber band, and note from where Joe had set them down on a cocktail table and walked over to her. "This is what broke the window, with the note wrapped around the brick and secured with the rubber band. We went over and picked it up so we could read the note. Other than that, we haven't touched anything. I also talked to the guy working behind the counter in the grocery store. He says he was wearing earbuds and listening to music at the time, so he didn't hear the window break, but he might have seen a suspect come in before the incident. He can give you a description, but it's kind of vague. Also, the security cameras in the store are fake, so that's a dead end."

Smart raised her eyebrows and looked over at her partner. "I see. Well, thank you for helping us out, Mr. . . . ?"

"Hardy. I'm Frank Hardy. This is my brother, Joe, our friend Charlene Vale, and our teacher Jane Havrilla."

"I took some photos right after the brick came through," Charlene offered, "if you need them."

"Sure, we'll keep that in mind," Detective Santos said. Charlene narrowed her eyes. The way he said it bugged me, too. It was condescending.

The crime scene techs came in and started taking pictures, dusting the doors for prints, and picking things up with gloved hands and putting them in plastic bags marked EVIDENCE. One of them came up and held out a hand for the brick and note, which I handed over.

Ms. Hawking started micromanaging the CSIs who were collecting evidence, demanding that they treat every shard of glass with the utmost care.

"We're going to need to interview each of you," Detective Santos said. "Smart, you start in here, I'll go talk to the guy in the shop, okay?"

His partner nodded, and he made his way out of the museum and back through the phone booth.

"All right, I'm going to talk to you one at a time," Detective Smart said. "Frank Hardy, why don't you come sit in this booth over here and tell me what happened?"

The others sat down at the big booths off to the side, and I settled into the booth Detective Smart had indicated, on the other side of the room.

"Okay. Now, you said you and your brother are here with a teacher. Is this some kind of school trip?" she said, flipping open a notepad that reminded me a bit of Charlene's.

"Yes, we're here with the Bayport High School History Club. There are fifteen of us on the trip, and three chaperones. We're visiting for the weekend."

I told her about discovering the documents in the tunnel yesterday and looking over the ledgers today with the curator and Mona. Then I recounted the whole story about the crash and finding the brick and questioning the guy in the shop.

"There are three colleagues at three different places that Ms. Hawking consulted about the documents. You should probably interview them, too, to see if they told anyone else about the discovery," I said.

"Mm-hmm, right. Will do. You may find this shocking, Frank, but as a professional detective, I do know how to work a case. We'll take it from here." She looked up from writing something down on her notepad and really studied me for the first time, scrutinizing my face. "Do I know you from somewhere? Where did you say you're from again?"

Suddenly I felt like I was on thin ice. "From Bayport," I said.

"Hmm," she murmured, looking like she was trying hard to place something she almost remembered. I was relieved when she finally told me I could go and sit with the others and to send Mona over to talk with her.

I slid into the booth next to Charlene and across from Joe, then told Mona it was her turn next.

"How did it go?" Joe asked.

"Fine," I said. "I just told her what happened. I think she might know who we are, though. Or recognize our names or something."

"That's probably not great," Joe said. "They might not like us being involved with their case."

"They can't exactly stop us," Charlene said. She may have been harboring a tiny bit of resentment from earlier. "At this point, we know more about the story than they do. We can help, whether they want to admit it or not."

I caught them up on my conversation with the guy in the store until Detective Santos came back into the speakeasy. He stepped around the crime scene techs and went to talk to his partner. After a couple of minutes, he looked up at us.

"Hey, kid! Hardy! What's your father's name?" Santos asked.

Oh man. "Fenton Hardy," I said. "Why?"

"You're one of those boy-wonder detectives, aren't you? I've heard about you and your brother, sticking your noses into cases where they don't belong." *Uh-oh.*

He strode across the room, right up to the booth. "Let me make something very clear. Maybe down in Bayport, you can get away with Sherlocking around and trying to show up the local police force. But that's not going to fly here in New York City. You're going to need to keep out of this case from now on and stay with your school group. Go back to touring the Statue of Liberty or whatever else you kids came here to do. Got it?"

I could practically feel waves of anger radiating off Charlene next to me. It never ceased to amaze me how territorial and threatened adults could get about Joe and me looking into these mysteries. As long as we didn't get in their way, how could it not be helpful? If they were so good at their jobs, why were they worried about us?

"Got it," I said mildly. I patted Charlene's arm, in what I hoped was a way that said, *I know, this guy is the worst. I'm sorry.*

Santos stalked off to interview Ms. Hawking across the room. His partner was approaching us, with a still-sniffling Mona in tow. Charlene stood and took a slightly crumpled pack of tissues out of her purse and offered them to Mona, who gratefully accepted.

Detective Smart seemed almost sheepish when she got to our booth and looked at us. "Here's my card," she said, handing it across the table to me. "You kids call me if you remember anything else."

She handed one to Mona as well. "We're going to catch whoever did this. And we don't take threats like this lightly. We're assigning a squad car to sit outside the grocery for the rest of the day and evening, to keep an eye on things. The officers won't let anything else happen to you." For all her big-city-cop gruffness, Smart seemed genuinely compassionate talking to Mona, who smiled weakly.

"Thank you, Detective." Then she blew her nose.

Detective Santos was walking back across the room with

the curator, saying, "I think you should remove the documents from the premises and keep them in a safe-deposit box. Ideally, cease your research on the discovery until the culprits behind the vandalism and threat are apprehended."

Ms. Hawking's face hardened into a picture of determination. "Detective, I've dedicated my life to uncovering the true history of this place and the organized crime operations behind it. These documents may very well be the biggest discovery of my career and change everything we thought we knew about that history. Respectfully, it's going to take more than a brick and an anonymous threat to stop me."

DIGGING UP THE PAST

7

JOE

AFTER WE LEFT THE MUSEUM, MS. Havrilla insisted we stop for coffee at a local, hipstery spot called Grounds for Celebration. She got a large latte, which seemed like the last thing she needed, considering how jumpy she was after the incident at the Top Hat.

We'd planned on spending much longer at the museum, and the rest of the club would still be on their tour of the Met. Ms. Havrilla wanted to meet up with them, probably so she could be relieved of the burden of being in charge of us, but we convinced her to let us go to the famous Stephen A. Schwarzman Building of the New York Public Library, a place Ms. Hawking had mentioned earlier, with the twin lion statues outside.

"It's quiet and there's air-conditioning and we'll just sit at computers and do research," Charlene reasoned. Ms. Havrilla could hardly argue with that.

We took the train uptown to Bryant Park and walked to the library. Inside, the main entry foyer was huge, with high ceilings and shiny floors and staircases on either side that were all completely made of white marble. It was one of those places where you felt like you had to whisper. There weren't signs or anything; it was just unspoken.

"Let's go upstairs to the Rose Reading Room," Charlene whispered. "There's Wi-Fi."

We followed her up and eventually walked into the room, which had the fanciest ceiling I'd ever seen, with gilded molding and painted murals of skies and clouds. There were people everywhere, reading and typing at laptops and taking books off the shelves lining the walls. We found an empty table and parked ourselves at one end of it. Ms. Havrilla sat down a few seats away, which was surprisingly chill compared to her chaperoning style up until now, and told us she was going to read an ebook on her phone and to please not stray far.

"You know what's been bothering me all day?" Frank said to Charlene and me. "I just feel like I've heard the name Kensington somewhere. It's in my head and I don't know why."

"I mean, we've been talking about Richard Kensington since yesterday," Charlene said, pulling her tablet from her tote.

"No, not that . . . ," Frank said, clearly racking his brain. "Wait, wait, I've got it!" His eyes went wide and he started rummaging in his backpack. Then, triumphant, he came out with a balled-up piece of glossy paper. "It's the campaign ads we keep seeing!"

He smoothed out the flyer on the table and we all leaned over to look at it.

* TRENT KENSINGTON *
FOR MAYOR OF NEW YORK CITY

TRENT IS THE CANDIDATE OF EVERY WORKING NEW YORKER!

HE UNDERSTANDS OUR IMMIGRANT COMMUNITIES AND WILL WORK FOR YOU!

HE IS TOUGH ON CRIME AND WILL MAKE SURE THAT THE HONEST, HARDWORKING PEOPLE WHO KEEP OUR CITY GOING CAN SUCCEED!

"Oh, wow," Charlene said, breaking the silence after everyone read through the rest of the flyer. "Do you think this Kensington has anything to do with the Richard Kensington from the documents at the museum?"

"Let's look at his campaign site," I said. "Maybe he has more about his family history on there, since he seems to be positioning himself as a candidate of the working class and the immigrant community."

Charlene opened the internet browser on her tablet and

went to Trent Kensington's website. There he was, probably pushing fifty years old but still boasting a full head of bright blond hair without a gray in sight. He was standing with a smiling wife and two children who looked to be in their early twenties, all decked out in crisp, preppy clothes. They even had a golden retriever. His biography on the site said that he was an entrepreneur, like generations of his family before him, and had made his fortune building a real estate business from the ground up. It wasn't hard to find attack ads from opponents, though, reminding people that he had inherited massive amounts of family money that he was using to help fund his campaign.

There was a tab called *A Proud Legacy of Hard Work and the American Dream.* On it was a grainy, old-timey photo of a family in front of a shop and a story about how the Kensington family had immigrated to America with five dollars and a dream and opened a small tailor shop, where they all worked hard and saved their money for many years. Eventually, they went on to buy a run-down building and fixed it up to be rented out for retail with apartments above, which was the beginning of the Kensington real estate business.

"This doesn't give names for the people in the photo," Charlene noted. She pointed to the man in the photo, who was standing in front of the shop with a woman—presumably his wife—and two children. "I wonder if that's Richard."

"If he is," I said, "then Trent's great-great-grandfather might have been some kind of Prohibition gangster who made his fortune in bootlegging and smuggling. That would make it a bit ironic for Trent to insist he's tough on crime and have a whole page on his site about his family history and their honest, hard work."

"That could be pretty bad for his campaign, don't you think?" Frank added.

We all looked at each other. If this checked out, we'd just stumbled onto a serious, high-level scandal.

Charlene looked a little bit like it was her birthday. "This is a major scoop if we can verify it. I think we should split up and each work on a different topic. We can cover more ground that way."

Frank and I had seen her like this before when she was working on a story. She was in full-on editor-in-chief mode now, and there was no stopping this train.

"I'm going to go talk to the librarian and see if they have microfiche of newspapers from the twenties about the raid," Charlene said. "Maybe there will be something there the curator forgot to tell us that will make it clearer what happened that night."

"Can I borrow your tablet, Charlene?" I said. "I'll try to look into the Facchini family. I bet I can even find a picture of Nicky Facchini so we'll recognize him if we see him at the store. I'm great at tracking people down on social media." Seriously, if I knew anything at all about a person, even a couple of small details, I could find their profile without fail.

"What should I do, then?" Frank asked.

Charlene considered. "I think you should ask the librarians to help you find census records from the twenties so you can try to look up anyone living in Manhattan at the time named Richard Kensington. Once we find the right one, we can start tracing the family line forward and see if it connects with our mayoral candidate."

Ms. Havrilla was absorbed in the ebook on her phone and didn't seem to mind that we were all peeling off. Charlene and Frank headed toward the information desk, and I got to work on the tablet.

First I tried to find a website for the East 2nd Street Deli and Grocery, but it didn't have one. It did have a Facebook page, though, which featured things like pictures of weekly sandwich specials, news about sales on different items, and a posting about how last April, a lotto ticket purchased at the store won someone five hundred dollars. I clicked into the *About* section and saw that the page's administrator was someone named Nicky Facchini.

"Bingo," I whispered, clicking on the link. The page was private, but I could see the profile picture. I opened the photo and knew the face right away. It was the man from behind the counter at the deli who I talked to the first day we were at the museum and who Frank questioned this morning, after the incident with the window. The one who had seemed totally disinterested in talking to us, especially about the Facchini family's connection to the speakeasy. *His* family's connection. He certainly hadn't been very forthcoming about who he was.

After a while, Frank slid into the seat next to me, a few printed pages in hand. Charlene followed close behind, holding her phone.

"What did you all find out?" she asked, a gleam in her eyes.

"I found records for three Richard Kensingtons who lived in Manhattan at the time," Frank said. "I printed out all three, but the one I think is probably the right one is listed as being a tailor who worked in the East Village. But his primary address is up on Fifth Avenue. The librarian said that was a really expensive area, even back then. Which seems weird for someone with a working-class job."

"Suspicious," I agreed.

"He and his wife had a son and a daughter, but I wasn't able to find census records for them. Maybe if we can figure out whether the son and daughter had children, we can trace the line to the present."

"Good," Charlene said. "That's really great. I found a couple of articles about the raid. Apparently the speakeasy was targeted based on an anonymous tip, like the curator said. So that seems like a dead end; I'm not sure how we'd find out a hundred years later who reported it. The article says that Sal was in the grocery store and Gino was in the apartment above when they were arrested, so neither was actually inside the speakeasy, which is interesting. Maybe that's why they didn't have time to escape. It also mentions that the police discovered the door to the escape tunnel that night because it was ajar. To me, that seems like *someone* had used it and left in a hurry. Like they forgot to fully close it behind them. Right?"

"That's how it sounds to me. But if it wasn't the Facchinis who went into the tunnel, who was it?" Frank asked.

"That's what we have to figure out," Charlene said. "Joe, what about you? What have you got?"

I couldn't help but crack a smile; I was pretty proud of my social media discovery. "Well, I looked up the East Second Street Deli and Grocery Facebook page, and look who's the administrator."

I turned the tablet around and showed them Nicky Facchini's profile.

"That's him! From the store!" Frank said. "I knew he was acting weird."

"Well, that explains some things," Charlene said. "I'm sure he doesn't appreciate people coming around and asking questions about how his ancestors were arrested for organized crime."

"He was pretty vague about the guy he claims he saw come into the store just before the window got broken. And it's still hard for me to believe he didn't hear that glass break, even with earbuds in," Frank said.

"If it was a guy in a suit like he said, though, maybe it was a political type. Some kind of advisor or bodyguard or campaign professional. Maybe Trent found out about the documents and didn't want it all to come out," Charlene said.

"But how could Trent have known?" Frank pointed out.

We all considered this. He didn't seem like the type to hang out at the Department of Records.

"You know what?" I chimed in. "Nicky Facchini was right there when it happened. He would have had plenty of time to throw the brick, go back to his stool behind the counter, and settle in to act innocent and oblivious before Frank got out there to question him."

"Very true," Charlene said. "Logistically, that makes the most sense. But why? If the documents could possibly prove that his great-great-grandfather or great-great-uncle were innocent or at least not the sole masterminds behind the smuggling organization, why wouldn't he want that?"

We all sat and thought for a minute. It was a tough one to puzzle out.

"Well," I said, "he told Frank that he and his family didn't want to have anything to do with the museum. And the note said to let the past stay buried. Maybe he just wants it all to be over with so he can move on?"

It wasn't really a satisfying answer for any of us. It's hard to move on and forget about something when there's an entire museum dedicated to it just feet from where you work every day. I still had a nagging feeling that we were missing something.

"I don't know," Frank said. "But if his ancestors took the fall for someone else, someone whose family is still powerful and influential a hundred years later, maybe there's a reason he wants to let sleeping dogs lie."

A SHADOW IN TIMES SQUARE

8

FRANK

SATURDAY WAS OUR FREE DAY, AND Joe was beyond excited to go to Little Italy for some pizza. Personally, I'd been dreaming about a plate of arancini. What could be better than balls of cheesy rice and meat sauce with a crispy, deep-fried shell? It was going to be epic. We barely picked at the continental breakfast because we were saving ourselves for our feast later.

First, we were planning on heading to Times Square to soak up the atmosphere and see if we could score tickets to a Broadway matinee at the half-price TKTS booth. It was worth a shot! We'd just have to avoid those creepy costumed characters along the way.

The terms of our free day were that we had to be in groups

of at least two, and we had to get our plans approved by Mr. Lakin ahead of time. For once, Joe and I planned on being in total compliance with those conditions. No diversions.

"Joe, are you ready? I'm sure people are already in line at the booth!" Sheesh. Joe had been giving me grief for the past couple of days about taking too long to get ready, but this morning he was definitely the one slowing us down. When he finally came out of the bathroom and sat on the bed to put on his sneakers, I walked over to the room door and saw a piece of paper on the floor. Weird. I knew that sometimes hotels slipped a bill or receipt under the door on the morning of checkout. Maybe they got the date wrong and thought this was our last day?

I went over to pick it up and recognized the handwriting on the note immediately. It was the same large, bold block letters as the note around the brick at the museum. The words were practically shouting across the page: *STOP INVESTIGATING NOW OR YOU WILL BE SORRY!*

I opened the door and looked both ways down the hallway. But it was quiet and empty, so I went back inside.

"Joe, come over here," I said.

"Give me a break! I'm almost ready!" Joe said, irritated.

"No, look." I walked over and held the note up in front of him. "Someone pushed this under our door."

Joe dropped his shoelaces and took the note. "It's the same handwriting as the one at the museum." He paused. "How did this person know where we're staying? Like, down to the exact room?"

We both absorbed this. Who would be able to track us down so quickly? And when did they leave the note? While we were sleeping? Sometime this morning? It gave me the creeps.

"Something tells me Nicky Facchini doesn't have the connections he'd need to get this kind of information," I said. "Is it time to tell Mr. Lakin?"

Joe looked back at me, a bit guiltily. "He'd probably make us all go home early. That would suck for everyone. And we'd never figure out the case. I know it sounds bad, but we've gotten threats before."

"We could give the note to those police detectives. And they can fingerprint it and keep it as evidence," I offered.

Joe nodded. He took the plastic laundry bag the hotel had provided out of the closet, and we carefully put the note into it, then tied it shut. I slipped it inside a notebook to keep it from getting wrinkled and put it in my backpack. "We can stop by their precinct later. It's downtown, on the way to Little Italy."

"Perfect. It's decided," I said, trying not to feel bad for keeping our teacher in the dark.

"Let's get out of here," Joe said. "All of a sudden, being in this room makes me feel like someone is watching me."

I had to agree with him there. We left the hotel and hopped a train to Times Square, 42nd Street. Coming out of the subway was an overstimulation explosion. There were hordes of tourists, massive TV screens playing ads, people dressed as superheroes and Disney princesses, vendors selling hot dogs and pretzels and glow sticks, and even someone painted silver from head to toe and standing completely still, pretending to be a statue.

The Times Square subway station was huge, and Joe and I had apparently chosen an exit that was blocks away from the discount ticket booth, so we had a ways to walk to get there. We stopped in at the M&M's store and grabbed a free sample of their new marshmallow flavor, which I thought was kind of weird. Joe loved it. We looked over the drawings on display at a caricature artist's stand, which were actually pretty great. He was drawing one of a little girl as we watched and had given her giant, anime-style eyes and ears that stuck out a bit. She seemed thrilled.

The whole time, I had that weird, nagging, itchy feeling on the back of my neck like someone was right behind me. I kept looking around and sometimes, I almost caught a glimpse of someone who seemed like they were watching me. But they always disappeared as soon as I looked back, sinking into the churning sea of bodies around us.

"Joe, I feel like someone is following us," I said, hoping I didn't sound paranoid.

"What?" he replied, turning from a street magician he was watching, who seemed to be levitating above the pavement.

"I keep almost catching glimpses of someone behind us, like they're following us. I think we have a tail."

Joe was immediately alert, scanning the crowd. That was

one thing I appreciated about my brother. He immediately believed me and took what I was saying seriously. "Do you think they've been with us since the hotel?"

"Possibly. Maybe whoever left the note was hanging around in the lobby or outside, waiting to see where we went."

"Well, if we can lose a tail anywhere, it's in Times Square on a weekend. Come on, follow me," Joe said.

He took off, weaving through the thickest clumps of people, going in and out of stores, zigzagging across streets. He was jaywalking with reckless abandon, and I had to jog to keep up. I kept scanning the crowd around us and yep— for sure—there was the guy. Suddenly it seemed like he was everywhere at once, moving quicker than was possible in the crowds. So there might even be multiple guys. Dark jacket, which was weird considering how hot it was, black hat pulled down low, and sunglasses. Generic secret-agent-spy wear.

"Joe," I said, panting slightly, "this guy is good. He's still with us. What do we do?"

"We have to . . . ," Joe started, then took a breath as we darted into the shop at Bubba Gump Shrimp Co. "Go somewhere he can't follow. But where?"

My heart was pounding. If this guy or guys caught up to us, what were they going to do? At this point, they'd definitely realized we knew they were following us.

"We could try to hop on a subway just as the door is closing. That works in movies," I said.

"Too risky," Joe countered. "If they make it on, we'll be stuck in an enclosed space with them."

"True," I said as we burst out the door of the shop and back into the crowd. Through the din outside, I heard the sharp *ding ding* of a bicycle bell. I stopped and did a quick one-eighty, then spotted it. A bicycle rickshaw was parked on a side street. I'd never been on one of these, but I'd seen them barreling down the street. Some of these guys were maniacs, weaving through traffic, ringing those bells, and shouting at cars for getting too close to them. I'd even seen one of them brandish a rock at a driver who cut him off. But maybe that was exactly what we needed right now.

"Joe! Over here!" I made a break for the rickshaw, Joe close behind me.

"Hiareyoufree?" I said, spitting it all out like one word, breathless.

"Hop in," the guy said in a thick accent that I recognized as "Brooklyn" from TV.

We did. "Can you please get us out of here as quick as possible? Just anywhere, whatever's fastest. If it's a street with a lot of traffic that a car can't get through, even better."

The guy raised an eyebrow but shrugged. "Sure, but it's cash only and I charge by the minute."

"That's fine, just please go!" Joe said.

"All right, all right, keep ya shirt on!" the guy said, pulling away from the sidewalk. He quickly picked up speed and merged in between the two lanes of cars that were stopped at a red light, driving on top of the dotted white lines, which seemed like a terrible idea.

I looked back, and two men in dark jackets were standing on the sidewalk where the rickshaw had been parked, watching us pedal away. I knew there was more than one guy after us! One of them was holding up an arm to hail a cab. My heart was pounding in my chest, but our driver was already zooming across the intersection against traffic, dodging cars like this was a game of *Frogger*, and soon the men were out of sight.

"Phew, I think we lost them," Joe said, catching his breath. "We owe you one, buddy."

"No, right now you owe me six fifty," he replied.

I was so tense and out of breath, I felt like a rubber band that was overstretched, and I just started laughing. It wasn't even that funny, but I couldn't stop. Eventually, Joe was laughing too, and the guy even chuckled a little.

"So, where are you two actually trying to go?" the guy asked.

I looked at Joe. "Pizza?"

He frowned. "Sadly, I feel like we should probably go to the museum and talk to Ms. Hawking. Things are escalating. We should warn her, in case she has people following her too and she just hasn't noticed."

I nodded. "Can you take us to East Second Street and Avenue A?"

So Joe and I were going . . . a bit rogue from our registered itinerary of Times Square, Broadway, and pizza.

"Sure thing," the guy said. "That's mad far, though. Cash only."

I rolled my eyes at Joe. "Yeah, you said. Don't worry, we're good for it."

9

FRENCHY AND "THE KILLER"

JOE

UR RICKSHAW DRIVER TURNED THE corner onto East 2nd Street, and man, this dude had some admirable stamina on a bike. That was a long, long ride. As soon as we were headed down the street, we could see flashing red and blue lights up ahead.

"Is that where you two are headed?" the guy asked. "Looks like trouble. I, uh . . . might drop you here, if you don't mind. I don't exactly have a permit."

"Yeah, that's okay," Frank said absently, already craning his neck to see what building the police cars were parked in front of. We paid the rickshaw driver a pretty hefty amount of cash and he pedaled away. Then we set off down the sidewalk, running toward the East 2nd Street Deli and Grocery.

Sure enough, there were two police cars double-parked right in front of it. We went inside and there was Nicky Facchini behind the counter, reading the newspaper again. So apparently the police were not here about something to do with his store.

"Hey, Nicky, what happened? Why are the cops here?" I asked.

He stood up behind the counter, putting his newspaper down. His eyes narrowed. "I don't think I gave you my name."

"You didn't," I said. "But that is who you are, isn't it? Nicky Facchini? Why were you so evasive before, when we asked if you knew anyone in the Facchini family? What would have been the harm of just introducing yourself?"

"I don't even know who you kids are; I don't owe you anything. And besides, like I said, I don't want to be involved. Sometimes history's better just left alone. We're over it."

Frank looked at me pointedly. That sounded an awful lot like what was written in the note that was attached to the brick.

"Well, unfortunately, it seems like someone isn't 'over it.' Was there another vandalism incident at the museum?" I asked.

Nicky shrugged. "All I know is someone broke into *my* store last night to get through to that museum. And now I have to pay for a broken padlock and security grille and have cops traipsing through here all day, scaring off business."

It was clear we weren't going to get much more out of

him. Frank and I made our way back to the phone booth and both doors were open; there was no need for the secret phone number today. We walked in and I got some serious déjà vu. Ms. Hawking and Mona were sitting in one of the red velvet booths. Detective Santos was on his cell phone in the corner, talking to someone, and Detective Smart was talking to the two women.

There was something major that was different, though, and it was impossible to miss. On the big mirrored wall behind the bar, in huge, glaring red letters, was the message, *YOU WERE WARNED. STOP NOW OR ELSE.* It looked like it had been written with spray paint; even from here, I could see drip trails of paint running down from some of the letters. No wonder poor Mona was crying again. This was some serious escalation.

A floorboard creaked when we walked in, and they all looked up.

Detective Smart looked supremely frustrated, like *Seriously, why do I have to put up with all this crap today?* "What are you boys doing here? I thought we told you to stay out of this."

"We were just coming around to share some research we did with Ms. Hawking. What happened?" I asked.

"Someone broke into the museum during the night and wrote that on the wall and stole all the documents!" Mona exclaimed.

"Which wouldn't have happened if you'd put them in a

safe-deposit box like I said," Detective Santos asserted from across the room. Man, that guy had an attitude problem.

"I needed them here so I could study them. They were no use to me in a safe-deposit box," Ms. Hawking said, her voice clipped. "And pardon me, but didn't you say that you had a squad car outside to keep precisely this kind of thing from happening?"

"Unfortunately, our night shift officers were called away briefly for a disturbance over at the East River Park. Bad timing," Smart said.

"Are you sure it was a coincidence?" I asked.

"What, you think it was a distraction?" she replied.

"Well, it could have been. Worth looking into, I'd say," I said. "Actually, while you're here . . ." I took off my backpack. "We had some excitement of our own this morning." I took out the laundry bag and handed it to her. "Careful, it's evidence."

She rolled her eyes at me, then opened it up and looked over the note, holding it out so Santos could see it too.

"Where did you find this?" she asked.

"It was slipped under the door of our hotel room. Somehow, whoever is doing this knows where we're staying," Frank said.

"Have you two been posting on social media a lot during the trip? Writing about the discovery at the museum? Or maybe you took a selfie in front of your hotel or even your specific room?" Smart asked.

"No, nothing like that. We've been pretty focused on this case," Frank said, then looked like he regretted it. "Not that we've been spending all our time investigating or anything."

"Well, someone thinks you are," Santos said. "We're taking this note into evidence."

"Also, earlier today we were in Times Square and there were a couple of guys following us. They seemed like professionals; it was really hard to lose them," I said.

"Are you sure?" Smart said. "There's so many people up there, it's tough to even stay with your group, let alone tell if someone is following you or if you're just repeatedly seeing different people around you who look similar."

"We've been tailed by shady people before," Frank said. "We know the difference between that and just being in a crowd."

"Okay, well, what did these mystery men look like?" Santos asked.

"We didn't get a really good look," I said. "They were in dark jackets, hats pulled down over their foreheads, and sunglasses."

"Right," Santos said. "Well, Ms. Hawking, I think we have everything we need here. There's another squad car outside to watch the door. Call us right away if you receive other notes or communications from these people."

"And please, stop digging into these documents for now. Obviously, it's dangerous," Detective Smart added. "That goes for you boys too. Let it go."

Once the officers had left, Ms. Hawking collapsed into the velvet booth next to Mona with a sigh. "Well, that's that, I suppose. I had most of the documents scanned, luckily, but not quite all of them."

"Charlene took a lot of pictures of the documents when we were here yesterday. If you give us your email, we can send them to you," Frank offered.

Her face lit up. "Oh, thank you, Frank—er, Joe—I'm sorry, which one are you?"

"Frank," he said.

Mona handed him the museum's business card so we'd have their email address.

"I'm sorry you've become involved in all this. It's certainly gotten out of hand. I never expected—well, things that happened a hundred years ago are immediate and important to a historian like me, but who would have thought there was someone out there who was willing to go to these lengths over them?" she said, sounding like she was on the verge of becoming distraught. She was still dressed fashionably, in an expensive-looking blouse, her unique glasses, and large, bold earrings, but everything was slightly disheveled: her bob frizzy, blouse rumpled, glasses askew. I would imagine this was very much not the norm for her.

"Getting involved in situations like this is kind of our thing," I said. "We're used to it. Actually, we did a bunch of sleuthing into these things yesterday and came up with some interesting information."

Frank and I showed Ms. Hawking and Mona the copies of the census records for Richard Kensington.

"Well done. I identified the same man in my own census research. I agree, a Fifth Avenue address for a tailor is very odd. Very suspicious," the curator said.

Then we told the two curators about Trent Kensington: what we found on his campaign site and our hunch relating to him, which got a big gasp.

"That's a serious accusation, you two. Quite a leap, based purely on a name," Ms. Hawking said.

"And his ancestor's profession," Mona asserted. "Both tailors, according to the census records and the campaign site."

"It's not an accusation yet," I said. "Just a hunch." Then I summed up Charlene's research from the microfiche articles. "Did you ever think maybe the fact that the hidden door to the tunnels was ajar and the car was missing meant that someone else had escaped from the speakeasy that night? Someone who knew about the exit when, possibly, the Facchinis didn't?"

Ms. Hawking considered. "Well, certainly I've wondered about those details. The Facchini brothers weren't *in* the Top Hat that night, so I always assumed they just didn't have time to get to the tunnels. Obviously, I never entertained the notion that the people I thought were at the top of the smuggling operation and speakeasy didn't know about the tunnels. There would have been employees working in the speakeasy that night, running the operations. My educated guess was that if anyone left through the tunnels, it would likely have been a person—or several people—who was lower down in the operation, like a bartender. I worked very hard for a while to find out who, but there just wasn't enough documentation. That is, until you fell right into some." She sighed. "Of course, now it's missing."

"But we did make some discoveries before it was stolen," Mona reminded her. She turned to us. "Some of those pages that looked like journal entries were actually letters written by a person who went by 'Duke,' talking to an investor about buying into the speakeasy. Part ownership. They were negotiating terms.

"Now, I suppose 'Duke' could have been one of the Facchinis, but we've never heard that name associated with either of them. Or if 'Duke' was someone else, perhaps the person he was corresponding with might have been someone in the Facchini family. Since Sal and Gino were renting the retail space in the front for their grocery store and were complicit in laundering the money from the speakeasy, maybe they wanted a bigger part in the business. That makes the most sense to me. But the letters are addressed to someone referred to as 'Frenchy.' We've never seen Sal or Gino called by that nickname either, and we don't know of anyone involved in the organized crime surrounding the Top Hat who was French. Everyone we've identified was Italian."

"But," Ms. Hawking asserted, "we know that Gino was stationed in France during World War I. It's possible he spoke some French or picked up that nickname due to that experience."

Frank and I looked at each other. The plot was thickening!

Ms. Hawking looked slightly comforted. "Yes, you're right to be excited. It's an intriguing development and opens up a lot of new questions and avenues for research. And we have something else to show you! Just a moment."

She scooted out of the booth and went to her office, then returned a minute later with a copy of a photograph, as well as a manila envelope. "I asked my friend at the New York Public Library for help finding old photographs of anyone who might be named Richard Kensington. She was able to uncover this in their collection of historical photographs." She showed us the photo and pointed. "We think this is the man we identified as Richard Kensington, from the census records." She then pointed to a second man in the photograph, who was standing next to Richard, with his arm draped over his shoulders in a chummy sort of way. He had heavy eyebrows and a cleft chin and wore a suit and fedora. "And this man is Owney 'the Killer' Madden, a notorious kingpin of the underworld during this time period. He's probably best known as the owner of the Cotton Club, but he also ran a large operation smuggling Canadian whiskey into the United States."

"Do you think he was a supplier for the Top Hat?" I asked, picking up the photo for a closer look.

"It's certainly possible. The Gilded Top Hat was known for signature cocktails that featured Canadian whiskey, so we know they were getting it somehow. I've spent years researching the Facchini family's associates and correspondence, trying to figure out who their connection was for the smuggling. But now it seems the connection wasn't theirs at all; perhaps the smuggling connection was Richard Kensington's, through Owney Madden," Ms. Hawking said.

"This is huge for us!" Mona said, leaning in conspiratorially. "I've already started planning where we can blow up and hang the photo in the museum."

"Let's not get ahead of ourselves, Mona," Ms. Hawking said, but for the first time this afternoon, she was smiling. "Of course, all this is confused by the other new piece of information we just received." She held up the manila envelope. "For years, ever since I started researching the Gilded Top Hat, every resource I've seen has said that the tip leading to the raid was anonymous. But when I came in and checked the mail this morning, there was an envelope in our mailbox—no postage, so it was hand delivered—containing this."

She opened the envelope and placed a piece of paper in a plastic sleeve on the table. It looked to be very old and was a typewritten report on some kind of police letterhead about the raid. Mona leaned over Ms. Hawking excitedly and pointed to a line near the top. "Here, look. There's a name listed for the person phoning in the tip—Richard K.

If the document is genuine, then it's possible Richard Kensington, the man from the deed, phoned in the tip about the speakeasy. Maybe as the landlord of the building, he legitimately wasn't involved in the criminal activities and didn't want them on his property. It's all so confusing—but exciting, too! We're sending the document to our chemist friend for historical analysis to make sure it's actually from the time period."

"Do you have any kind of hunch about who delivered the police report?" I asked. "Where would someone even get something like that?"

"I honestly don't know," Ms. Hawking admitted. "I haven't been able to obtain a historical police report like that about the raid. I was led to believe such a document didn't exist. I do wish the grocery store had actual security cameras! Clearly, it's time to think about allocating some of our budget to them. Money has just always been so tight. Perhaps we could apply for a grant. . . ." She trailed off.

"Well, we have a tour of the National Jazz Museum tomorrow that's all about the Cotton Club," Frank said. "Maybe they'll know some things we don't about Owney Madden. Can I take a picture of your picture?"

"Be my guest," Ms. Hawking said. "And please do let me know what you find out. I have to admit, you boys may have a future in curation and historical research after all."

THE POLITICAL THIRD RAIL

10

FRANK

"JOE, I KNOW WE MEANT TO GO GET pizza," I started.

"I know, I agree, we need to keep at it," Joe said. "There is a time for pizza, and there is a time for sleuthing. And this is the latter."

I smiled. "Very mature of you."

"This might be a bad idea," Joe went on, "but when we were researching Trent Kensington yesterday, I saw on his website that his campaign headquarters is in the West Village, and today volunteers are gathering there to do door-to-door campaigning. What if we show up? We can ask people around the office about the candidate's background and connections. You know, just to be informed. In case voters ask when we knock on their doors."

I couldn't help but smirk. It was a very Joe plan. "I like it. Let's go." We started walking across town toward the subway station. "You know who would be really good at this?"

"Let me guess. Your girlfriend?" Joe teased.

"Cut it out, Joe. Charlene and I . . . she's not my girl-friend," I said. I mean, truthfully, I was hoping that's where things were headed. Charlene was awesome. But Joe didn't need to make it weird. "She is great at this kind of thing, though. She knows just the kinds of questions to ask people to get information out of them."

"Do you know what she was planning on doing today?" Joe asked.

"Not sure. I'll text her," I said. I was pretty sure she was part of a larger group that was going to the Museum of Modern Art with Mr. Milstein, but I was willing to bet she'd ditch for this. She could be as . . . flexible as we were about rules when an investigation was at stake. Besides, a group of three is safer than a group of two, right? Mr. Lakin would probably agree to that one point, at least.

It was only a minute or two after I texted Charlene about our plan that my phone pinged from my pocket with a text back.

Charlene: I love an undercover mission. ;) Send me the address and I'm there.

Despite being farther away, Charlene somehow beat us to the campaign office and was standing in front when we got there, sipping an iced coffee.

"Hey," I said. "Man, you got here fast."

"Express train, slowpokes," she said. She held out her drink like she was offering it to me. "Maybe you need some caffeine, Hardy. Gotta be on your game for this. We're about to touch the political third rail in there."

"Third rail?" I said, scrunching up my eyebrows.

"Yeah, like on the subway. That's the rail that's electrified, that can kill you if you touch it. Just like the topic of Kensington's ancestors' criminal activities, if he's not careful."

Of course Charlene knew some random, obscure political lingo.

"Okay, well, Operation Third Rail it is, then," Joe said. "Ready to go?"

"Maybe we should all go in separately. Just, you know, to be subtle about it," I suggested.

Charlene nodded. "Okay, me first. Then you two come in staggered by a few minutes."

Before either of us had a chance to respond, she slipped into the campaign office and was gone.

"All right, boss! Got it!" Joe muttered.

"Oh, come on," I said. "Man, now I wish I had iced coffee. It's hot out here."

After a few minutes, Joe went inside. I waited a bit longer, pacing back and forth on the sidewalk around the corner. When I couldn't take it any longer, I went in.

The front room of the campaign headquarters was packed with people of all ages, standing in clumps, wearing buttons and T-shirts with Trent's face on them. To my right was a registration table, where a woman stood up to greet me and asked me to fill out a sign-in sheet with my name, phone number, and email address.

I froze for a second, not having prepared anything, then wrote, *Chet Milstein, cmilstein2023@gmail.com, 555-5050*. I looked farther up the list, and Charlene and Joe had come up with much better names and phone numbers, which didn't seem quite as fake as mine. But I'd already written this one, so I was committed. I handed back the paper and luckily, the woman didn't even look at it. She handed me a button, a pile of glossy flyers, and a map, with a number of blocks highlighted in yellow.

"These are the blocks you're assigned to," she said in a sunny voice. "Once the orientation session is over, you can head that way. There will be several other volunteers assigned to those blocks as well, so you won't be on your own."

"Okay, thanks," I said, taking the map. Then I walked away and did my best to disappear into the crowd. I spotted Charlene and Joe but tried not to acknowledge them.

It seemed like we'd arrived at the right time, because an energetic, smiley woman was stepping up to a microphone at the front of the room and tapping on it twice with her manicured nails. It gave off two muffled *woomp* sounds.

"Is this thing on?" she said, her voice resounding through the room. The chatter started to slowly taper off. "Hello, all you wonderful volunteers! Welcome to the campaign headquarters for Trent Kensington, our great city's next mayor!"

There was cheering and whooping from around the room. After basking in it for a few moments, the woman raised her hands for everyone to quiet down. "Today we are going to get out there to talk to our neighbors and help this city's undecided voters become part of the Kensington crew! Trent wanted me to thank each and every one of you from him, personally. He isn't able to be here today, but we have an exciting speaker to go over talking points with you. I'm here to introduce our top campaign manager, the man with the plan who is steering our ship, Mr. Paul Vander!"

More cheering filled the room as the woman stepped aside, and up walked a man I remembered from the photographs on the website. He'd been in a lot of them, usually standing behind the candidate with a leather portfolio or handing him a microphone or a bottle of water. He was shorter than he had looked in his photos, with dark brown hair that was slicked back with so much hair gel it practically looked wet. He had quick gray eyes, and even though he was smiling broadly, something about him felt standoffish.

"Thank you, thank you. Everyone quiet down," he said. "Before you go out to talk to voters, I'm going to give you a run-through of Trent's background and platform, as talking points." There was a whiteboard behind him, and as he talked, he took a thick black dry-erase marker and made notes about his main ideas for everyone to see.

"Trent Kensington is a native New Yorker whose family has been in Manhattan for generations. He knows this city and knows its people because he is one of them. His great-great-grandfather immigrated to the United States with five dollars and a dream"—*Man, how many times had we heard that phrase?*—"and started a tailoring business that he used to pull himself up by his bootstraps and make his fortune, eventually moving into the real estate business. Trent is a candidate who understands the American Dream and the value of hard work. He is an advocate for the working class here in New York City. The issues that are important to the immigrant community are also very important to him. He is tough on crime, especially white-collar crime, and will fight to keep dishonest people from getting ahead while the good, hardworking—"

"Excuse me?" A hand rose from the sea of people in the crowd. "I have a question."

I would know that voice anywhere. What was Joe doing?

"I was just wondering. I've heard some rumors, probably put out by other candidates, that some of the Kensington family money wasn't come by through such honest, hard work. Is there any truth in that?"

I dared to look over at Charlene out of the corner of my eye, and she had her hand over her mouth. Third rail! Third rail!

Paul Vander raised an eyebrow and stared down into the crowd, still smiling widely. He craned his neck slightly, as if to get a better view of who was speaking in the middle of the sea of volunteers, but he couldn't seem to fix his eyes on Joe.

"Well, there are always attack ads during any campaign. But if it happens to come up with a prospective voter, you can feel free to tell them it's pure fiction. Everything the Kensington family owns has come from honest enterprise, from his great-great-grandfather's tailor shop to the real estate empire that Trent has built from the ground up."

"Right, of course," Joe continued. "But I heard a rumor that Mr. Kensington's great-great-grandfather was involved with bootlegging and smuggling, and that the Gilded Top Hat speakeasy was run out of a building he owned. What should we say if someone asks about that?"

Mr. Vander was still searching the crowd for the speaker, but he maintained a very stiff smile. "Well, since I'm his campaign manager and I've never heard these shameful lies, I doubt a voter will ask about them. Mr. Kensington's ancestor owned many buildings in his time. If there had been crime happening in one of them and he found out about it, he would have reported it to the authorities. Now, as I was saying—"

Just then his eyes rested on Joe and his entire demeanor changed. He glared down at him, frowning, and tensed up his posture. "Anyhow, the rest of the talking points are in the flyer. Now let's get out there and connect with some voters!"

The peppy woman who had introduced Vander let out a "Wooo!" and burst into applause. The crowd was slightly tentative, but after an awkward moment, they started cheering as well, and the mood felt more relaxed as everyone gathered in groups to set out on their routes.

I slowly moseyed across the room to stand near Joe and talk to him without facing him. "What was that, Joe?"

"I thought I would catch him off guard, in public, and it would be harder for him to lie. Maybe he'd let something slip. I figure none of the other campaign workers here know anything significant. I mean, those people at the check-in table and the microphone just don't seem like they're in the inner circle, you know?" I could practically hear him shrugging.

"I see what you mean," I conceded. "I doubt anyone below his level on the campaign knows much. But so much for being subtle!"

"He knew exactly what I was talking about when I brought up the Gilded Top Hat. Did you see that? He recognized the name," Joe said.

I peered across the room, and Vander was having an animated conversation with a couple of huge, surly men. Then he looked toward us, and before I could turn away, he'd made direct eye contact.

"Joe," I said under my breath, "I think we have a problem."

Vander pointed across the room at us, and the two men, who I now saw were wearing black shirts with the word SECURITY across the front, started coming right for us.

"Oh no," Joe said. "Walk away, Frank. They're probably

just going to kick me out, and you and Charlene can stay and collect information."

But when the men reached us, one of them grabbed each of us by an arm.

"We have enough volunteers for today," one of the men said in a low grunt. "It's time for you two to leave."

They escorted us out, not roughly, but firmly. People stared as we crossed the room. We passed by Charlene, who was having a conversation with a young woman in a baseball cap and a T-shirt with Trent's smiling face on the front. She glanced at me out of the corner of her eye and then went back to her conversation. Good. At least one of us would be able to stick to the plan.

Once the two of us had been pushed out the door and it had been shut behind us, we regrouped. After a moment, my cell phone pinged.

Charlene: Yikes. Sorry you two. I'm going to stay with the group and gather intel. Meet back up later?

I texted back: Yep, be careful.

A moment later, another *ping*. Charlene: I'm not the one that just got manhandled by security lol

She had a point.

"Well, what do we do now?" Joe asked. We started walking down the block, away from the campaign office.

"You know what's been bothering me?" I said. "How did whoever is threatening us and the curator know about the papers and the research? Who leaked that information?

Ms. Hawking was pretty emphatic that it wasn't one of her colleagues. I figure someone must have overheard their conversation."

"So we try to figure out where and who?" Joe said.

"That's what I'm thinking. Want to start with the Department of Records she mentioned? I'm sure a lot of people come in and out of there every day."

"Okay, let's do it."

We were heading down the block toward the subway station to hop a train downtown when I got that prickly feeling on the back of my neck again. I slowed on the sidewalk and grabbed Joe's arm to slow him, too.

"Hey, let's take a selfie," I said.

"What?" Joe said in disbelief. "You want to take a *selfie*? Right now?"

I leaned in next to him and turned the camera so it was facing us, then aimed it between our heads so I could see behind us. Sure enough, there was a man in a dark jacket and sunglasses lingering half a block behind, scrolling through his phone and trying to look like he was just leaning against the steps of a brownstone to take a little break.

"Don't turn around, but we're being followed again," I said.

Joe looked at the screen of my phone. "He must have been tailing us since the campaign headquarters. What do we do?"

"We're only half a block from the train station. I think

we need to have our MetroCards ready and we need to run. And hope there's a train waiting on the platform."

"I told you that's a bad idea that only works in movies. What if there isn't a train?"

"Then I guess we're out of luck. Unless you have a better idea," I said hopefully.

Joe thought for a moment. "Unfortunately, I've got nothing."

"Okay then. Got your MetroCard?" I said.

"Yeah, in my back pocket."

"Hold it in your hand and run when I say go."

He nodded.

"One . . . two . . . three . . . go!" Both of us started sprinting down the block, shoes slapping on the pavement. I was so, so glad I hadn't decided to wear flip-flops today. A moment later I could hear pounding footsteps behind us, but I didn't look back. I know from unfortunate experience that when you look back during a chase, you usually end up falling on your face and getting caught. Not today!

Panting, hearts racing, we got to the corner and saw those round green lights marking the subway entrance. We barreled down the stairs and by some miracle, I could hear the rumbling of a train coming down the tracks.

"Get your card, Joe!" I shouted.

"I know!" he shouted back. He got to the turnstile first and managed to swipe and get through almost without breaking stride.

I ran up, swiped my card, and crashed into a stationary turnstile that smacked me right in the gut. What? My card had money! It did!

I looked at the little screen on the turnstile. *Too fast. Swipe again at this turnstile.*

My pulse thundered in my ears. The train was sitting in the station now. Joe was halfway onto the train, holding the door. I could hear footsteps on the stairs, getting closer.

I swiped my card again, slower, and the turnstile still didn't budge. *Swipe again at this turnstile.*

I let out a frustrated "Ughhhhh!"

The train conductor was shouting at Joe over the loudspeaker, telling him to stop holding the door. I swiped one more time. The machine beeped and the turnstile turned. I ran through so fast I tripped on my own feet and practically fell into the train. The door shut right behind me, just as the man in the black jacket ran onto the platform.

We watched him pass by out the train window as we sped off into the dark tunnel, catching our breath.

DETECTIVES OF TOMORROW

11

JOE

WE FINALLY GOT OUT OF THE train downtown in the Financial District and headed to the Department of Records and Information Services Municipal Library. It was a very grand building, with three arches at the entryway, a row of columns up above, and a blue roof with ornate granite decorations. It was such a stark contrast to the sleek, angular glass skyscrapers that were all around in the area.

I still couldn't quite believe we'd managed to shake the tail. Frank kept scanning the crowds around us reflexively, searching for anyone who looked like they were watching us. It seemed now that the surveillance was probably coming from the campaign after all. Clearly, they were not pleased that we were looking into these things.

We went into the building, and there was a directory hanging on the wall. It listed a department called *Historical Records—Genealogy*.

"I bet that's who Ms. Hawking was talking to," Frank said. "Trying to get information on Richard Kensington."

I nodded. "Let's go talk to them."

We found the office and walked in to find two middle-aged women in glasses and cardigans behind desks, clacking away at computers. One of them was carefully flipping through an old book with yellowing pages, looking from the computer to the book and back, as if she was transcribing information.

They looked up when we came in, and the one closer to the door smiled and said, "Hello, welcome. I'm Ethel. Can I help you two with something?"

"Hi. Yes, we're hoping you can," I said. "We've been working with Ms. Hawking from the Prohibition Museum on some new research she's doing. She said she was here a day or two ago."

Ethel's face lit up. "Oh yes. Jennifer was here looking for records from the twenties. Naturally."

"Do you keep a log of everyone who comes into the office, by any chance? Like, a record of people who make inquiries or request historical documents?" Frank asked.

She raised an eyebrow. "Well, we don't have a sign-in sheet, if that's what you're asking. But if someone requests access to records on a certain day, we'd be able to look that up in the system. Why?"

"We're trying to figure out if anyone was here at the same time as Ms. Hawking, who may have overheard what she was talking about that day. I'm not sure if you've heard, but there was a break-in at the museum and someone is making trouble relating to what she was researching," I said.

"Yes, the police were here to speak with me. It's all so terrible," she said. She paused, looked from Frank to me and back, considered. "I'm sorry, I may have forgotten if you already told me this, but did you boys say who you are? I didn't know Jennifer had interns quite so young at the museum."

"Uh," Frank started.

"We're with the NYPD Detectives of Tomorrow program," I said. "We've been paired with Detectives Santos and Smart to shadow them on their cases. That's why we've been working closely with Ms. Hawking. To figure out what happened to her missing documents."

"I've never heard of that program," Ethel said. "How interesting. Do you have documentation?"

I searched my brain for any possible excuse as to why we didn't have a shred of proof about this made-up program.

"Well, since we're basically NYPD junior interns, they can't issue us official ID," Frank said, picking up the slack. "But Detective Smart gave me her card to show, in case anyone asked." He handed over the detective's crumpled business card from his pocket. I held my breath.

The woman looked it over. "They really should give you some little badges or something. It would be nice," she said, but she handed back the card and seemed satisfied. "I can tell you what I told them, which is that I would never betray Jennifer's trust by telling someone else about her research. Neither would Agatha." She tilted her head over to the woman at the other desk. "We're very discreet. We're professionals."

"Do you remember what time Ms. Hawking was here?" I asked.

"It was around five o'clock on Thursday. I remember because I was about to go on my dinner break. There are reruns of *Downton Abbey* on at that time, so I like to watch them in the break room. But I was happy to miss the beginning of the episode for Jennifer."

"Was anyone else in the office at the time?" Frank asked.

Ethel looked up and to the right, like people do when they're trying to remember something. "Well, I'm not sure. There might have been someone here. People come in and out all day. Anyway, she asked me about the person from her research, that Richard, um . . ." She leafed through some papers on her desk, as if looking for the answer.

"Kensington," I said.

"Right. Kensington," she confirmed.

"Did you say Richard Kensington?" Agatha said, looking up from her yellowed book at the other desk.

"Aggie, I just finished telling these young detectives that

we're discreet, and now you're listening in on our conversation," Ethel chided.

"No, but I know that name. I just pulled records on that person the other day," Agatha said. "I wouldn't say anything normally, but if it's a police matter, that's different."

I could feel my heart rate quickening. Someone else was looking into the case. "Do you remember what day that person was here looking for those records?" I asked.

Agatha tapped on the keyboard with her manicured nails for a bit before she said, "He requested the records last week but came to pick them up late in the day on Thursday."

"Does that mean this person could have been in the office at the same time as Ms. Hawking? Could he have overheard what she was telling Ethel about her new discovery?" Frank asked.

"It's possible," Agatha said.

"Do you have a name for the person who picked up the records?"

"Sure, it says . . ." Agatha typed some more and her face fell. "Oh, it says 'Elvis Presley.' I suppose that's . . . not the person's actual name."

I did a quick Google image search on my phone and pulled up a photo of Trent Kensington. "Agatha, this is really important. Was it this man who came to pick up the records?" She looked at the phone and shook her head. So I went to Facebook and pulled up the photo of Nicky Facchini from his profile. "Was it this man?" No again.

"Do you remember anything about what he looked like?" Frank asked.

"Well," she said. "Not handsome like that first man. Or young like that second man. He was maybe fifty or so, sort of stocky, with brown hair. A bit brusque, impatient, you know? At least, I think I'm picturing the right man. Like Ethel said earlier, a lot of people come through here."

I looked over at Frank, and he seemed to be deep in thought. "And you said 'Elvis' requested the records *last* week?" She nodded. I turned to Frank. "That's way before we discovered the hidden documents in the tunnel. It doesn't make sense."

"Someone already knew," Frank said.

"Can we possibly see the records you provided to the King of Rock and Roll, Agatha?" I asked. "It could be really helpful to the case."

Luckily, Agatha laughed. "Well, if it's for the NYPD. And to help Jennifer and the museum." She did some more typing, and then the printer across the room whirred to life.

When it was done, I grabbed the still-warm pages from the tray. "Thank you both! This is so, so helpful."

Outside, we sat on a bench with hot dogs from a street vendor, since we both finally realized we'd skipped lunch and were starving, and looked through the papers. They were detailed genealogical records tracing a family line from

Richard Kensington, the Fifth Avenue "tailor" who went on to own the building containing the Gilded Top Hat speakeasy, straight forward to—there it was—Trent Kensington, real estate mogul and mayoral candidate. There was no question. This was the politician's dirty secret.

"So who figured it out before the documents were even discovered? A political rival?" Frank asked.

"Maybe," I said. "But if an opponent had information this harmful, you'd think they would put it out right away. The election is only a couple of weeks from now. There isn't really time to play a long game."

"And it wasn't Nicky. So who—"

"Hey, it's Nicky!" Frank said.

"Agatha said it wasn't," I reminded him.

"No, look, across the street. Nicky Facchini," Frank said, pointing. "Maybe we should ask him about all this, since we ran into him."

I slipped the papers into my backpack and we jaywalked across the street to where Nicky was walking by. He had his earbuds in again, so Frank had to walk in front of him and then stop short to get his attention.

"Hey, tourists, I'm walkin'—oh, *you*. What do you want with me? I'm busy," Nicky said, looking suspicious and annoyed as soon as he recognized us.

"Did you hear that someone stole a bunch of newly discovered documents from the museum? They're documents about someone named Richard Kensington, who looks like he might actually have been the owner of the Gilded Top Hat," I said.

"Yeah, so?" Nicky said, trying to sidestep Frank.

"What do you mean, 'Yeah, so?'" Frank said. "It's possible that this person was the main smuggler and criminal boss behind the speakeasy, not your ancestors. It could mean the wrong men went to prison."

"That's not news to me, kid. My family's been telling people that for decades. No one wants to hear it," he said.

"Did you ever have proof before, though?" I asked.

"You know what proof I have? My family was completely broke after Sal and Gino went to prison. They lost the grocery business, obviously, and their wives and kids ended up in the almshouse on Welfare Island after they went away. Do you know what that means? It means they were locked up because they couldn't pay their debts. You can look up the records. They didn't have any secret, hidden bootlegging money. My father and I only recently built the business back again when that retail space went up for rent."

Frank and I looked at each other. "But they must have known about the speakeasy," I said. "All the money was being laundered through the store. And besides that, there must have been tons of drunk people wandering in and out through the telephone booth at all hours of the night."

Nicky finally stopped trying to get around us and looked at me. "Yeah, of course they knew. They weren't idiots. They were renting their store from the guy who owned the building. I guess that was the guy who ran the speakeasy. What are you gonna do, tell your landlord what he can and can't do on his own property? I have some old letters Sal's wife wrote to a cousin about it. They were behind on rent and the guy said he'd kick them out unless they either paid, with interest, or fixed their books to hide the speakeasy's profits and make it look like the store was earning this extra money. That's how they survived and kept paying their rent. In discretion and money laundering."

"You have proof of this?" I asked, excited. "Why didn't you ever show Ms. Hawking?"

"All I have are a couple of old letters from Sal's wife, like I said. They don't even mention the landlord's full name—they just call him 'Duke.' It sounds like Sal didn't really tell her much about it." Nicky ran a hand through his hair and sighed. "Why am I even telling you all this?"

Frank and I both looked at each other immediately. Duke! The landlord—Richard Kensington—was "Duke" from the letters!

"But why have you been so evasive and unhelpful? If what Ms. Hawking is doing could clear your family's name once and for all, don't you want that?" Frank asked.

"My grandpa spent his whole life trying to prove that his grandfather and great-uncle were innocent. He was obsessed. It took up all his free time. And he could never do it. It was the disappointment of his life. So I just don't care anymore, okay?" Nicky said. "What I care about is figuring out how to keep my store in business. I'm down here to go to the bank to apply for a small business loan. That's what I want. You two can run around and play detective, but leave me out of it." With that, he pushed past us and disappeared into the crowd on the sidewalk.

Frank and I just stood there for a moment, absorbing what we'd learned. "So Richard Kensington was 'Duke,' who *definitely* owned the Top Hat and was looking to sell part ownership. According to Nicky, the Facchinis laundered the money, but that's it. They weren't involved with the operations of the speakeasy," he said.

"I guess Gino could still be 'Frenchy' from the letters, like Mona and Ms. Hawking were guessing. But it makes more sense to me for them to have been scapegoats," I replied. "If they weren't actually a part of running it, then they wouldn't have known secrets like the location of the escape tunnels. It sounds like on the night of the raid, they were left to just take the fall. With all the financial records about the money flowing through their store, it was an easy conclusion for the police to come to. Not to mention the fake deed that Kensington must have left for the police to find."

"But then what about the police report listing the person who gave the tip about the speakeasy and smuggling operation as 'Richard K.'? Why would he report his own operation? Unless it's completely random that the name of the person who tipped off the police is so similar?"

"Nah, that seems like too much of a coincidence," I said,

shaking my head. "But I'm still not a hundred percent sure I trust where that document came from. Why couldn't Ms. Hawking find it before?"

Frank chewed his lip like he did when he was thinking hard. "I don't know. But I do know it sounds like Nicky really doesn't want to be part of any of this. I believe him," he said.

"Yeah, me too. But someone was looking into these things, even before the documents were found. And if it wasn't him and it wasn't Trent, we still have to figure out who and why."

TRADING IN SECRETS

12

FRANK

WHILE JOE AND I WERE STILL NEAR the Department of Records, Charlene called to let us know she was done with her canvassing and ready to meet up. We got together in Washington Square Park.

"How was it with the campaign?" I asked.

"It was interesting. After that campaign manager kicked you out, I tried to find out as much about him as possible. It turns out this guy Paul Vander is a big deal. Super high-powered. He's done campaigns for senators, governors, and other mayors. He's won nearly every race he's ever worked on, and he has a reputation for using whatever tactics are necessary," Charlene said. "I'm talking attack ads on other candidates, dragging skeletons out of their closets, questionable fundraising strategies, possible bribery, you name it. Most of that is only rumor, of course. He's never been officially accused of any misconduct. And his candidates always keep their hands clean."

"I bet his services don't come cheap," I said.

"Definitely not," Charlene agreed. "I heard him talking about how he thinks Trent could be president one day. And I'm pretty sure he wants to be a presidential campaign manager turned presidential advisor someday. He's ambitious. Not that ambition is bad. I'm ambitious. But he gives me very cutthroat vibes, you know?"

"Well, I certainly got a cutthroat vibe when he was ordering his cronies to kick us out of the campaign office," Joe said.

"That's another thing. I'm sure he's dealt with less-than-flattering questions about his candidates loads of times in much more public settings than that room. He was getting this question from a teenager, with no press present. And at first, he didn't actually seem so bothered. But it was almost like, as soon as he saw you, something changed. I know it doesn't make sense, but it was almost like he—"

"—recognized Joe," I finished. "I knew something was bugging me about it. And that's what it is. It's like he saw Joe and immediately wanted him out. He even cut the presentation short to do it. And why kick me out too? We were being careful not to make it look like we were together."

"Apparently he recognized you both," Charlene said. "What did you two do after you got ousted?"

We told her about the tail from the campaign head-quarters, our trip to the Department of Records, and the encounter with Nicky Facchini.

"I'll bet your Elvis Presley is some campaign underling sent out by Trent to pick up that stuff," Charlene said.

"But why would he be researching his own family history? Don't you think he already knows?" Joe asked.

We all looked at each other, stumped.

"That part is kind of odd," I said. "But the rest of the evidence all points to him. The genealogy records confirm that Trent is related to Richard. And every historical record we've seen clearly shows that Richard Kensington owned the Gilded Top Hat. Plus, we know that the campaign is having us followed. The tail originated from the headquarters."

"I bet they're behind the threats, too. They wouldn't want this to get out. I think we need to talk to the detectives before this gets any worse," said Charlene.

"We can try," said Joe. "But based on our experience, they might not want to listen to what we have to say."

I shrugged. "We aren't all that far from their precinct. It's worth a shot."

When we got to the busy police precinct, we walked in and asked the officer at the desk in front to speak to Santos or Smart, showing him Detective Smart's business card. He had another officer walk us back to a desk where Detective Smart was sitting behind a computer, walled in between stacks of file folders.

She looked up and instantly seemed annoyed. "Ah, the Scooby Squad. What are you doing at the precinct? We're busy here."

"We have a lot of evidence to share with you that's relevant to the museum case. It all implicates Trent Kensington or someone on his political campaign. We think it's a cover-up—" Joe started.

Detective Smart was already shaking her head. "Listen, we've looked into this."

"But just look at what we have!" Charlene cut in. She laid out the files from the Department of Records and pulled up the photo of Owney Madden on her phone, then recounted the story of the Facchini letters, even though from her, it was thirdhand. Charlene had some serious gumption.

"And this will all be thrilling for your history project," Detective Smart said, when Charlene slowed down. "But we've been doing police work. I shouldn't share information on an open investigation." She pursed her lips. "But we've checked alibis and cleared his senior staff. They can prove that the candidate's ancestor reported the smuggling; he didn't commit it. So there's no cover-up. We're almost ready to close the case now, with an actual suspect. You kids just go back to your field trip. If you interfere more, we might have to consider obstruction charges. I'm serious." Smart was getting up from her chair. She flagged over a younger-looking officer. "Hey, Officer Meagher, show these three out."

Once we were on the sidewalk, Joe let out a frustrated sigh. "I saw a copy of that historical police report on her desk, with the tipster listed as 'Richard K.' The campaign must have given it to her, and she's convinced."

"That probably means they were the ones who sent it to Ms. Hawking, too," Charlene said. "If so, I'd bet money it's fake."

"Guys," I said, with dread in the pit of my stomach. "There was something else on her desk. She had an arrest warrant for Nicky Facchini."

"What?" Charlene exclaimed. "But we know he didn't do this!"

"Ugh," Joe said, shaking his head. "I mean, to play devil's advocate for a second, the police could say that he was there when the first incident happened and has a pretty weak excuse for not seeing or hearing anything. And for the second incident, he had keys to get into the store and could have broken into the museum with some degree of privacy, then tampered with his own security grille for show. Even though it's circumstantial, he had opportunity."

"But he's having financial problems," I asserted. "He was complaining about the cost of fixing the grille. And the motive makes no sense! If anything, he would want all of this to come out. It clears his family and implicates the Kensingtons."

"Not if the police believe that report about 'Richard K.' calling in the tip. The campaign basically convinced the detectives they aren't concerned about any accusations because they have proof of Richard's innocence, and therefore they don't have a motive to make threats," Joe said.

I looked from Joe to Charlene. "If we want to show the detectives that Trent does have motive, we're going to have to prove the report is fake. I think we'd better try to figure out who really called in that tip, and fast, or an innocent man is going to jail—again."

On the way uptown to Harlem in the morning, Charlene, Joe, and I sat and stewed in silence, trying to figure out where we could even start looking for a historical document about an anonymous tip to police that even Ms. Hawking had never been able to find.

No one had come up with anything by the time the train had rumbled its way uptown and Mr. Lakin led us all off onto the platform, then up to the street. We walked down West 129th Street until we got to a redbrick building with a brightly colored sign on the side that said THE NATIONAL JAZZ MUSEUM IN HARLEM.

When we filed in, we were met by a woman wearing a dress in a print that looked like music notes. She ushered us into a large room filled with chairs and told us that she'd be giving us a presentation about the Cotton Club.

She projected a PowerPoint, and a slideshow of old black-and-white photographs started: a marquee with COTTON CLUB in huge letters across it, with old-timey cars pulling up in front; a crowd of glamorously dressed revelers under an arched ceiling; musicians playing onstage; and a lineup of dancers in flashy costumes. Upbeat jazz played quietly in the background.

"The Cotton Club was a legendary nightclub here in Harlem that operated between 1923 and 1940," she said. "Over the years, many of the greatest Black musicians of the era performed on that stage, including Louis Armstrong, Billie Holiday, Duke Ellington, and Lena Horne. The club was a popular, fashionable meeting spot, but it had a segregated policy, so initially Black people were not permitted to patronize the club. The talented Black musicians played for white audiences at a club where they themselves would not be welcome as guests." She clicked the remote in her hand to advance the slides. "A very select few Black customers were allowed to visit the club, including Harlem Renaissance poet Langston Hughes. After his visit, he called the Cotton Club 'a Jim Crow club for gangsters.'"

Charlene raised her hand. "We heard that it was run by a gangster. Someone named Owney 'the Killer' Madden?"

The woman smiled at Charlene. "Yes, that's right. Owney Madden was a bootlegger and gangster who purchased a club called the Club Deluxe and renamed it the Cotton Club after he got out of prison in 1923. He partnered on it with a former gang rival, George Fox De Mange, also known as Big Frenchy."

All three of us stared at each other, eyes wide. Frenchy!

The person referenced in the letters, who was looking to acquire partial ownership of the Gilded Top Hat, must have been Big Frenchy De Mange, Owney Madden's partner. It definitely wasn't Gino, regardless of where he'd been stationed during the war. That last question mark about the Facchinis' involvement was gone now. They weren't potential partners. They were just left holding the bag, like Nicky said.

"Excuse me," I said, raising my hand. "Did Owney Madden and Big Frenchy make a habit of acquiring clubs or speakeasies, beyond the Cotton Club?"

"Oh, definitely," the woman said. "They owned or had investments in more than twenty nightclubs across the city. That also included the Stork Club, which was the stomping ground of infamous gossip columnist Walter Winchell. Maybe you've heard of him?"

Charlene was nodding vigorously. *Of course* she had.

"As a journalist, he was extremely well connected in the Prohibition-era underworld. Sometimes he traded in information, sometimes he was paid off for his silence. He supposedly once said, 'I usually get my stuff from people who promised somebody else that they would keep it a secret.' A nightclub was certainly a prime location to collect gossip! But anyway, back to the Cotton Club. In 1925 the club was briefly shut down by police. . . ."

I tried hard to pay attention, but my mind was on overdrive, connecting all our pieces of evidence. There was the deed listing Richard Kensington as the owner of the building;

the ledgers that could be matched to his handwriting; and the letters with the "Duke" nickname (which could be verified by Nicky's family letters), where he offered part ownership to two gangsters, Madden and De Mange. But those had all been stolen from the museum, almost certainly by the Kensington campaign, and were likely destroyed by now. We had scans or photos of some, but would that be enough? There was also the photo of Richard and Madden, plus the genealogy records. Those were from undeniable sources. But then there was the police report, which implied that Richard found out about the speakeasy on his property and reported it himself. That report was almost definitely falsified, but if the tip was actually anonymous, how could we disprove the narrative the campaign had created? I didn't know how long historical document chemical analysis took, but we probably didn't have time to wait for Ms. Hawking's colleague to study the document and decide whether it was genuine. The police were bound to make an arrest anytime now, if they hadn't already.

When the presentation was finally over, Charlene came over to Joe and me on the sidewalk outside the museum.

"Frenchy!" she exclaimed.

"I know! So that's it. Madden and his partner were thinking about buying part ownership of the Gilded Top Hat. I guess after supplying whiskey for a while, they saw how successful the speakeasy was," I said.

"I think we should follow up on Walter Winchell,"

Charlene said. "I've studied him in my journalism courses. He knew everything about everyone back then. If Richard Kensington was involved with Madden and De Mange, maybe he even knew Winchell. Maybe he hung out at the Cotton Club or the Stork Club. I . . . um . . . During the presentation I ducked out to 'go to the bathroom' and looked up places to do research on him. It turns out the library has a huge archive of his personal notes and papers here in Manhattan, at the Billy Rose Theatre Division. I bet if we ask Mr. Lakin, we can convince him to let us go."

I couldn't help but smile. Once Charlene was onto a story, she had blinders on. The itinerary for the trip was totally out the window.

"All right then," I said, feeding off her excitement. I had a good feeling about this. "Let's go see what people told Walter Winchell after they promised they'd keep it a secret."

DROP DEAD LIST
13

JOE

MR. LAKIN JOKED THAT WE WERE basically on our own separate trip at this point, since we asked to go to Lincoln Center Plaza and visit the theater library instead of the club's next planned stop, but he seemed undeniably proud that we were so enthusiastic about historical research. And Mr. Milstein did us a solid by saying that it would be great for us to visit another branch of the New York Public Library and that he wanted a full report afterward. Librarians for the win!

We went up to the information desk to speak to the librarian in front, and Charlene took the lead. "Excuse me, hi," she said. "We were wondering if we might be able to look at the Walter Winchell papers? We're doing a research project about his connections with Owney Madden and Big Frenchy De Mange."

"Oh, how interesting!" the librarian said. "Well, usually we require researchers to request those kinds of materials beforehand."

"Oh." Charlene's face fell. "I understand. It's just that we're on a school trip and we're leaving tomorrow. It would be so amazing to see the papers in person! I've read about the collection online and it sounds incredible."

Flattery. There ya go.

"It really is," the librarian said. "Well, I suppose I could expedite the process, just this once. Which papers were you hoping to look at?"

Charlene gave a radiant smile. "Oh, thank you so much! We'd love to see Series One: Personal Papers, if that's possible."

The woman gave a conspiratorial smile. "Now, you three just wait right here and I'll see what I can do." Then she headed off through a door marked STAFF ONLY.

"Wow, Charlene, nice one!" I said. "I was worried there for a minute."

"I've spent a lot of time doing research in libraries, and if there's one thing I know about librarians, it's that they really love helping people find resources and access information. Especially if you ask nicely," she said.

Soon the librarian came back with a large box and set us up with it in a private room. She gave us all white gloves to wear, even though the papers were in plastic sleeves, like the ones at the Prohibition Museum.

"Please be careful with the papers and put them back in an orderly fashion when you're finished. And return them to the desk before you leave."

"Of course," I said. "Thank you so much!"

"My pleasure," she said with a smile.

We set to work, looking through notebooks and letters and columns. There were all kinds of letters, some from celebrities whose names I recognized. It was hard not to get distracted reading things that had nothing to do with the Gilded Top Hat or Richard Kensington.

Finally I got to a piece of paper with notes on it that looked like a grocery list. I almost couldn't believe this warranted preservation in a plastic sleeve in a fancy archive at a library, but then I turned it over and froze. On the back of the sheet, written in fading pencil, was a scribbled note that started with, *Gilded Top Hat.*

"Guys!" I said. Charlene and Frank put down the papers they were looking through. "I found something."

They came over and huddled around me. The century-old pencil was hard to read, but it was there: *Gilded Top Hat, RKT, DDL, Apr. 8, 2 a.m.*

"I can't believe it!" Charlene said. "This is for sure about the speakeasy!"

"Yeah, but what does the rest of it mean?" Frank asked.

"Okay, well, it's the location. Then, hmm . . . RKT?" I said, racking my brain about the letters.

"Maybe they're initials? Like, Richard KensingTon?" Charlene suggested.

"Yeah, could be!" Frank said. "So, the bar and the owner. Then what? What's 'DDL'?"

We were all quiet for a few minutes. "Well, the rest is a date and time, obviously," I said.

"Wow, Joe. Genius!" Frank teased. "I feel like that date and time ring a bell, for some reason."

Charlene picked up her phone, and her fingers started flying across the screen. "Aha! I knew it. Look." She turned the screen so we could see. "That's the date and time the speakeasy was raided."

"Whoa," I said. "I wonder when he wrote this. Do you think he knew about the raid ahead of time?"

"I think we need to know what 'DDL' means," Frank said.

"Hold on, I'll get our librarian friend," Charlene said. She came back in a couple of minutes with the woman from the desk, who looked almost as excited as we were.

"See, here it is," Charlene said. "That's the name of the speakeasy and the time of the raid. But what does 'DDL' mean? Do you know?"

"I do, actually!" the librarian said. "Walter Winchell was known for being somewhat volatile, even vindictive. He kept track of his grudges on something he called the 'Drop Dead

List.' The people on the so-called list were on his bad side. It seems like whoever is referenced here might have crossed him somehow. Does that help?"

"Immensely!" Charlene said. "Thank you so much!"

"Of course," the librarian said. "And thank *you*. I'll make a note about the meaning of that message. We hadn't put it together before."

She headed back to her desk and we all started to talk at the same time, then all stopped to let someone else speak, so there was just silence. Then finally I said, "So, do we think Winchell had some kind of beef with Kensington and reported the Top Hat to the police? So he was actually behind the raid?"

"If Kensington was on the Drop Dead List, then that seems likely," Charlene said.

"But I guess it's also possible that Winchell found out about the raid somehow and was the one to tip off Richard Kensington so he could get out in time before being arrested," Frank guessed. "Although then the DDL part doesn't really make sense."

"*Or,*" I said, "this might be a stretch, but hear me out. Maybe Winchell tipped off the police to cause a raid, and then he traded the information about when it was going down to Madden for a payoff or something, since he knew the Killer was investing in the bar. Winchell doesn't seem like the kind of person who would give away something for nothing. And creating a run-in with the police so that he could trade a tip-off about it to a gangster sounds like something he might do, just from what we know about the guy."

"Any of that could be true, for sure," Charlene said, laying the piece of paper flat on the table and taking photos of it with her phone. "If your theory is true, Joe, it would make sense how the information got to Madden and then to Kensington far enough in advance that he could leave behind the fake deed and get out through the tunnel. I just wish there was a date on it from before the raid, instead of a grocery list."

I laughed. "Any way we can figure out what day in April 1925 he ran out of milk?"

"Doubtful," Charlene said, with real regret.

"No matter which of these is true, this is some pretty good evidence that Walter Winchell may have phoned in the tip. That makes a lot more sense to me than Richard Kensington reporting his own speakeasy to the police," Frank said. "Do you think the police would take this as evidence that the historical report they have is falsified?"

"I hate to be a downer," I said, "but somehow I don't think this is going to sway the detectives. It's not a hundred percent solid. We should tell Ms. Hawking everything we found out, though. It'll be significant to her. She's going to totally lose it, in a good way."

I looked at my watch. "It's not too late in the afternoon yet; the Prohibition Museum should still be open. Let's call."

Frank dialed the number and put it on speakerphone. It was picked up after the first ring.

"Yes? Who is this?" came a forceful, sharp female voice that was definitely not Ms. Hawking.

"Uh, this is Frank and Joe Hardy and Charlene Vale. Is Ms. Hawking there?" Frank said.

"Seriously? You kids again?" There was a muffled conversation in the background. I caught a snippet of what was said. It sounded like, "No, it's the Junior Detectives Club on the line. Pain in my rear is what it—"

There was a sound like someone's hand over the speaker, then a male voice on the line. "Hardy, this is Detective Santos. Get off this line and do not call back. We're keeping it clear in case we get a call from a kidnapper. Goodbye."

"Kidnapper! Wait, wait, wait!" I said, spitting it out as fast as possible, hoping he wouldn't hang up. "What are you talking about? Who got kidnapped?"

"Jennifer Hawking. Last night," he said.

"Well, has there been a ransom note? Any demands?" Frank chimed in.

"No, which is why we need to keep this line open. Don't call again or I'm hitting you all with obstruction," the detective said. Then the call was disconnected.

DON'T BE LATE

14

FRANK

E TOOK THE TRAIN BACK TO THE hotel in shock, barely saying anything. It had all gotten so real. This wasn't just threatening notes or broken windows. A woman had been kidnapped.

During the train ride, I got an email notification and saw that one had just arrived with the subject line, *New Information/Please Be Careful*:

> Frank and Joe,
> I'm not sure if you know, but Jennifer has disappeared. We got word back from our colleague who specializes in historical ink that the police report was a forgery. Jennifer

was furious and decided to create a post on our website with all the new information, including the scans and pictures of the documents we still have, the photos of RK with OM, everything. Minutes after the post went live, the site crashed. Then she left for the subway to head home, and no one has heard from her since. My partner and I are leaving town. Please let this go and tell your teacher you all need to leave NYC now. I can't have you kids involved. I'm sorry.

Take care,

Mona

I passed around my phone so everyone could read the email. "That was a brave thing for Ms. Hawking to do," I said. "But clearly, someone from the campaign was watching the website, too. Not just the actual museum. We all agree that's who's behind this, right? To me, there's no other explanation."

"Absolutely. They have the motive and the resources to pull this off, and now their flimsy fake police report has been busted. I hope the detectives have cleared Nicky. There's no way they can think he did all this," Joe said.

"The police are waiting for a ransom demand that isn't coming—Kensington and his people don't want money. They want to shut Ms. Hawking up. But what are they going to do? Hold her hostage until after the election? Or . . ." Charlene trailed off. None of us wanted to finish her thought. Would they really go to such extremes? Finally she said, "Poor Mona. She must be terrified. She knows just as much as Ms. Hawking does."

We sat with that for a while. I hoped she and her partner were somewhere safe. I scanned the train around us. I hoped *we* were safe. There was no way of being sure anymore.

We stopped for fast food when we exited the subway, since lunchtime had come and gone. It was hard to be hungry, though, when there was so much going on with the case.

When we got back to the hotel, I asked Charlene if she wanted to come hang out in our room to make a plan.

"Sure," she said. "I really don't feel like watching reruns of *The Bachelor* with Sally tonight. I want to be doing something, you know? Maybe we can come up with something that will convince the detectives to seriously go after the Kensington campaign as suspects for Ms. Hawking's kidnapping."

"That's the spirit!" I said. Did that sound corny? I was pretty sure it did. But she smiled.

"I'm just going to go to my room to get my tablet and camera. I'll be back."

"Okay, see you in a sec," Joe said as he opened the door to our room.

As soon as we got inside and closed the door, I surveyed the disaster zone that was our hotel room. "Joe, I need you to stuff all that dirty laundry back in your suitcase ASAP, please! How did it get all over everything??"

I started darting around, picking up junk food wrappers and shoes and sunglasses. "Does it smell weird in here?"

"Dude, relax. It smells like a hotel room," Joe said.

Right. He was totally right.

It didn't take long for Charlene to knock on the door. I kicked one more empty water bottle under the bed and went over to let her in. She'd changed into a white hoodie and yoga pants, since the hotel was way over-air-conditioned, and she was carrying her tablet like a tray with her DSLR on top.

"Hey. Welcome to Chez Hardy," I said.

"Surprisingly clean," she noted approvingly. She plopped down on the edge of my bed. "So I was thinking, first we should email Mona back and make sure she gave the detectives the chemical analysis of that fake police report. That way, the police will know the Kensington campaign group gave them false information. That should at least cast some doubt on their credibility and bolster our evidence about their motive for all these crimes."

"I'm on it," I said, opening up a draft on my phone in response to Mona's email.

"You know what's been bothering me?" Joe said. "It's the last thing that doesn't fit. Why would someone from the campaign be looking up genealogical records about Richard Kensington at the Department of Records? Wouldn't Trent already know those things about his family? Why would they want to draw any kind of attention to that stuff, even from a librarian like Agatha? It doesn't make sense."

Just then, there was a quiet *slip* sound from behind me. I turned around toward the door and there was a piece of paper there, facedown, one edge still partway under the crack between the door and the floor. Someone had just slid it in.

I sprang up. "Another note!"

I grabbed it and flipped it over. As soon as I saw the bold, black block writing on it, I flung open the door, started running down the hallway, and shouted back, "Joe, Charlene, run the other way! We have to try to catch whoever left this!"

I could hear them running out of the room after me, then their footsteps fading down the corridor. I ran as fast as I could, with the paper in my hand whipping through the air. Hotel hallways are creepy. Door after door after door looked exactly the same, and so did the carpet and the light fixtures, so it almost felt like I was on a treadmill, not moving, just looking at the same room to my left and right.

Finally, I reached the end of the hall and got to a fork. Left or right? I made a snap decision to go right and almost collided with a housekeeper.

"Excuse me, I'm so sorry," I said, trying to catch my breath. "Could you please tell me if you just saw someone come down this hallway in either direction?"

"Oh, no," she said. "No one. Just me." Strangely, she seemed a bit out of breath too. There was sweat on her brow.

"Did you, by any chance, slip this under the door of 15E?" I held up the note so she could see it.

She looked sheepish. "A man in the lobby gave me a very large tip to bring it up. It was folded in half and he told me not to look at it, so I didn't. I hope it isn't anything bad or upsetting, sir. I didn't mean any harm."

"It's okay," I said. "The note isn't your fault. Do you remember what the man looked like? The one who gave it to you?"

She scrunched up her nose for a moment, thinking. "He was wearing a suit. Very nice black suit, expensive. Maybe designer. He was short and stocky with brown hair and dead, gray eyes like a shark. I hope that helps. I don't want any trouble."

"No, of course not, don't worry. Thanks for the information," I said.

I went back to the room, and Joe and Charlene were already back there, looking discouraged.

"No one!" Charlene said. "I don't know how they could be so fast."

"It was a housekeeper," I explained. "Someone paid her to slip the note under the door." I gave them the description.

"Well, that's not Trent," Joe said. "Hey, what does the note say? We didn't even look."

I unfolded the note that was crumpled in my hand and read, "'We have Jennifer Hawking. If you ever want to see her alive again, both of you come to the Gilded Top Hat in one hour, alone. Bring your phones, camera memory cards, and all other devices with copies of the documents on them. No police or Hawking dies. Don't be late.'"

"Oh my God," Charlene murmured. "This is so intense. What are we going to do? We have to call Detective Smart. We're in over our heads."

"These people said no police or else, and I believe them," Joe said. "They've already committed vandalism and harassment and kidnapping, you know? Who knows what else they're capable of if we don't do this how they want?"

"That's exactly why we need to tell the police," Charlene replied.

"Okay, wait, let's just think about this," I said. "There's three of us, and they only seem to be demanding that Joe and I show up. That's an advantage. Also, honestly, they don't seem to have a very good understanding of how the cloud works. We can hand over our phones and your memory card and we'll still have the files."

"All that tech is expensive," Charlene muttered.

"I think all three of us should head down there. Charlene, maybe you can hide out inside the grocery store or somewhere nearby. If we're not out of there in, say, twenty minutes, you can call Detective Smart. Does that sound reasonable?" I said.

Charlene thought about it. "Well, I don't love this plan. But okay. They said be there in an hour, so that means we have until"—she checked her phone—"seven o'clock. I think we should leave soon, just in case. Also, I've been working on writing an epic exposé about all this. It's almost finished. I think I'm going to draft an email with the article and scans of all the photos and documents and schedule it to be sent in, say, two hours to a whole bunch of New York media outlets. The *Times*, the *Wall Street Journal*, you know. That way, you can tell them that if anything happens to you and you can't get back to your hotel room to stop the email in time, it's going to auto-send. And you won't be lying."

"Good thinking," Joe said. "I like it."

"Okay, just wait a minute. I'm getting my backpack and I'll be back," Charlene said. When she returned a few minutes later, she handed me her camera memory card in a clear plastic case. Then she grabbed something else out of her backpack and gave it to me. "Here, take this with you. It's pepper spray. My mom gave it to me for the trip. Just in case."

"You are full of surprises, Charlene," I said, putting the small canister into my pocket. "Thanks."

"Are we ready?" Joe asked.

"As we'll ever be, I guess," I said. "Let's go find out who our pen pal is."

FIGURES IN THE DARK

15

JOE

WHEN WE GOT TO THE EAST 2ND Street Deli and Grocery, all the lights were off, including the neon OPEN sign. But the silver metal grille that should have been rolled down over the entrance after hours was up. A padlock that looked brand-new—presumably the replacement for the one that was destroyed in the last break-in—appeared to have been cut off, maybe by a bolt cutter. It was on the ground next to the shop door. Someone had broken into the shop again.

I stepped forward and gave the door a tentative push. It opened with a screech that made Frank flinch next to me.

"Jumpy?" Charlene whispered.

"Aren't you?" Frank asked.

"Yeah, I am," Charlene admitted. "This is all really stressful. We could still turn back."

I looked at my watch. "It's been an hour since we got the note," I whispered. "If we're gonna do this, we have to do it now. Let's go."

We all stepped into the store, and I made sure the door shut slowly and quietly behind us. We crept down the center aisle of the silent grocery store together.

"Charlene," Frank whispered. "Are you okay staying here? You've got Detective Smart's card, right?"

Charlene nodded her reply to both questions. "I'll have the number dialed into my phone and be ready to press send the second I hear something off or my timer hits twenty minutes. So if you're in trouble in there, just shout, okay?"

I nodded. "Thanks. We've got your pepper spray, so, you know, we can always spray any political henchmen in the face if they threaten us."

We all chuckled nervously.

"Okay, here goes," I said. "Come on, Frank."

He and I went back to the phone booth and tried the outer door, which opened. Ms. Hawking had had the lock replaced after it was pried open during the vandalism incidents. Now it looked like the shiny new lock had been unlocked with the actual key. Maybe the kidnappers forced her to open it or just took her keys from her. The hole where the stained-glass window used to be was covered in plywood and the back door was ajar, so I pushed it gently. The museum was pitch-dark. I fumbled around on the wall near the door but couldn't find any light switches, so Frank and I took out our cell phones and lit the flashlights, sending the beams out into the large space. It was hard to see anything inside, but the room looked empty. We'd just have to go in.

I stepped out of the phone booth into the room, phone flashlight held high, and Frank followed.

"Who's here?" I shouted into the darkness. "Come out and show yourselves! Ms. Hawking? Are you there?"

Frank put his back to mine and we turned around slowly, shining our flashlights all around us. The darkness shifted and moved, as if there were figures everywhere, but it was hard to tell if there were people or just shadows cast by the various display cases and pieces of furniture.

"Someone's here," Frank murmured, turning slightly toward me. "I swear I can hear them."

I wasn't sure if I could hear other people in the room or if it was just my own pounding heart and rasping breath.

"Turn on the lights and come out or we're calling the police!" Frank said loudly.

That was when we heard the door to the phone booth, which we'd left open, swing shut, and the lock engaged with a loud *click*. Then figures started to materialize from the shadows. I spun around, looking on all sides. There were so many of them, at least four—no, seven men around the room, closing in.

"Frank, we've gotta get out of here!" I shouted, hoping my

voice would carry out the door of the phone booth to where Charlene was hiding.

"How?" Frank replied, sweeping his flashlight around the room like the beam from a lighthouse, illuminating the men as they came closer and closer.

My brain raced. How, how, how? "The tunnels! Hurry!"

The two of us turned and sprinted toward the back corner where the hidden door to the escape tunnel was. There was a narrow pathway between two of the shadowy men where we could slip through to get there, but they were closing the distance quickly. For a split second, it looked like the two men were going to cut us off and block us from both sides, but as we got close, Frank whipped Charlene's pepper spray out of his pocket and doused the closer lackey with it. The man let out a bellow and took a few clumsy steps backward, tripping over his own feet. Frank stumbled over him and kept sprinting forward; I stayed hot on his heels.

We got to the corner where the hidden door was and skidded to a halt, then started frantically pushing on the panels, trying to get the door to pop open.

"Which one is it?" Frank shouted, panic quivering in his voice.

"I could have sworn it was"—I pressed down on a panel, hard, and heard a *pop*—"here!"

The door swung open and we both threw ourselves through it. I slammed it shut behind us as Frank started descending into the darkness. Once the door closed, I barreled down the spiral stairs so fast I was getting kind of dizzy. I clutched the railing, but even with the grippers on the steps, my feet were sliding and I knew I could slip and take a tumble all the way down at any second. I heard pounding on the door up above. Apparently, the lackeys up there were having trouble getting it open. Good.

As Frank and I descended, panting in the darkness and listening for footsteps behind us, I remembered Ms. Hawking's insistence that everyone wear hard hats in the tunnels. In the scramble to get down here, neither of us had taken one.

Once we got to the bottom of the stairs, there was at least some light dimly illuminating the tunnel. The work lamps were on, strung up along the dirt walls. We kept running down the passage, careful not to slip. We both still had our cell phones in hand with the flashlights on, so we used them to illuminate the dark corners.

"What do we do now?" I panted, my voice echoing through the tunnel.

Frank glanced at his phone as he ran. "No signal down here. Charlene should be calling the detectives soon. I think we need to just get as deep in as possible or find somewhere to hide out. Those goons will be on us any minute," he said.

"Okay," I agreed. "Good move with the pepper spray."

"Thanks," he said. "Hey, did you hear that?"

We were quiet for a moment, and then I heard it too. There was something that sounded like a faint shuffling and then a noise almost like an angry cat.

"Yeah, I did," I said. "I don't know what it is, but it sounds like it's coming from up here."

We passed by the armory room, and the noises got louder and started to sound more like muffled words.

"Okay, that is definitely a person," Frank said.

"Ms. Hawking?" I called out. The shuffling got louder. We kept running down the hallway and rounded the corner into the room with the plinth for the safe. Huddled on top of it in the dark was a wiggling figure. I shone my flashlight on the person and it was Ms. Hawking, with her hands and feet bound and a piece of duct tape across her mouth.

"Ms. Hawking! Are you okay?" I said as we ran over to her.

She nodded but strained against the bindings and let out a stifled shout that sounded a bit like, "Me out!"

"Don't worry, we're going to get you out of here," Frank said. "Hold still." Carefully, he peeled the duct tape off her mouth.

"Oh, thank you. Thank goodness you're here. Did you call the police?" Ms. Hawking asked, breathless.

"Charlene should be getting the police here right now," I said.

I took out the small pocketknife I kept on my keys and started cutting through the duct tape around her ankles.

"What happened?" Frank asked. "Who did this to you?"

"I—I'm not entirely sure," she said. "I left work yesterday and was walking to the subway to head home. Then all of a sudden, a van pulled up next to me on the street. It was one of those Mercedes vans, you know. A fancy one. A huge man in a suit opened the middle door and leaned out. He said he was trying to follow directions on the GPS on his phone, but they weren't making sense and would I take a look? So I went over to see, since I know the area so well, and he just grabbed me. Then there was something strange-smelling over my face and I don't remember anything else for a while. Then I was in a place that might have been a hotel room and someone kept asking me who I'd talked to about the documents I found. I told them everything they wanted to know. God, I hope they haven't gone after Mona."

The duct tape came off her ankles and I tossed it aside, then moved on to her wrists. "We got an email from Mona earlier today," I said. "She and her partner left town."

"Well, that's good," Ms. Hawking said.

"What did he look like, the man who was questioning you? Was he tall and blond?" Frank asked.

"No," Ms. Hawking said. "He was actually a relatively short man, stocky, with brown hair and gray eyes."

Something clicked into place. The description. It was so similar to the one that was given to us by the housekeeper at the hotel and by Agatha, from municipal records. Suddenly I knew who they were all describing. And the handwriting from the notes—it was his too. I had seen him writing before, with a black marker.

"Frank, I know who's behind all this. It's—"

Just then, something cracked me on the back of the head, hard, and everything went black.

SKELETONS IN THE CLOSET

16

FRANK

THINGS WERE FUZZY AND DARK. MY nose and mouth were squished up against something hard and moist and moldy-smelling. Wood planks. I was lying on an uneven, wet wood floor. Before I could see anything, I could hear someone humming in the distance, but it was getting louder; the sound was echoing strangely and it hurt my head. *Ouch.* Someone had hit me on the head.

I tried to move but found that my hands and feet were bound with something tight and sticky. More duct tape. I rolled over so at least my face wasn't on the ground. There was a dark lump lying next to me, still.

Joe. It was Joe. "Joe, hey, wake up," I whispered. I tried to scoot closer and swung both my legs together toward him, kicking his feet. "Hey, are you okay?"

He groaned. Phew. "What happened?" he said groggily.

"Someone knocked us out. Can you see Ms. Hawking?" I asked.

Joe paused. "I think I might see her over there."

We fell into a hush to listen. The humming continued down the tunnel toward us. The song sounded familiar. It was . . . "Hound Dog," by Elvis Presley. *Elvis.*

"Joe, do you hear that? The Elvis?" I said, hoping it made sense to him and he didn't just think I had a concussion.

"Yeah. Frank, I know who's been doing this. It's Paul Vander. All the witnesses have been describing him the whole time. His handwriting on the whiteboard at the campaign headquarters, it's the same as the notes. He's behind all of it."

The sound of someone slowly clapping broke the quiet in the tunnel like thunder, and I almost jumped out of my skin. "There you go! The boy detectives have cracked the case," a voice said, getting louder and closer. I rolled over to face where it was coming from and heaved myself into a sitting position. There, walking down the dimly lit tunnel with the light from the work lamps shining off his slick helmet of gelled hair, was the campaign manager.

"Unfortunately for you, you've done it just a bit too late," he said. I could see that he was holding both of our cell phones in his hand. He walked right up to me and held mine in front of my face, unlocking it. Then he started scrolling through. "I'm going to have to delete your camera roll, I'm afraid. And who have you been texting about all this . . . ?" He paused, reading. "I'll need to speak with this 'Charlene Vale.' I assume she's at your hotel. I'll send one of my associates to pick her up so she can join us."

"You won't find her there," I said hastily. "She's at the police station right now, talking to those detectives about you, so they'll be here soon."

Vander studied me for a moment. "You know what? I don't think she is. I think you're bluffing, young man."

"And you know another thing?" Joe chimed in. "She wrote a whole article, laying out our findings about Richard Kensington and the Gilded Top Hat and his connections with all those smugglers and gangsters. And she's sending it, along with all our documentation, to the *New York Times* if we're not out of here in the next ten minutes. So you'd better think carefully about your next move."

Vander laughed. He actually laughed, like one of those villains from a movie. "Well, I do have your phones. So how about this? You're going to tell her to hold off." He took my phone and started tapping on the screen, dictating what he was typing. "'We R OK. Found Ms. Hawking. Wait 2 call detectives and send article 4 now.' Problem solved."

"So just to recap," I said, because now the initial fear I'd felt was turning into anger, "your boss has been lying about his family legacy and he's hired you to cover it up, and so now you're guilty of, let's see, vandalism, harassment, breaking and entering, theft, document forgery, hacking, and multiple counts of kidnapping and assault. Is that seriously worth it? Just to get him elected? Don't you realize you're getting saddled with all the dirty work?"

Vander smirked. "Oh, but that idiot doesn't know about any of this. He actually thinks his family is the perfect embodiment of the glorious American Dream. Everything he says, he believes. That's why it sells. But I wouldn't be the best campaign manager in the business if I didn't know every single skeleton in my candidate's closet. Even the ones they don't know are there. So weeks ago, I requested everything they had on his family from the Department of Records. While I was waiting for that, I found out about all this bootlegging mess when I was going through family records at Trent's house, looking for material for that corny 'My Ancestors Were Hardworking Immigrants' page on his website. Nobody else seemed to know, and I was ready to bury it until I overheard that darned curator talking to the woman at the records office about discovering long-lost documents in a tunnel, of all places. There is no way she is ruining this for me. Or you two, for that matter. If some intimidation won't work, and a forged police report won't work, then fine. I'm in this all the way. Trent is going to become mayor of New York City. And then he is going to become president. And I'm going to be in his cabinet. If I have to squash a few scandals on the way up, that's perfectly fine with me."

Vander held Joe's phone up to his face to unlock it and started going through, deleting the camera roll and reading texts.

"There's no possible way you're getting away with this," Joe said. "Too many people know. The documents are out there. These aren't the only copies. The police are going to find us down here eventually."

Vander looked up from Joe's phone. He went over to a large, jagged rock, half-embedded in the dirt wall. Then he placed the phone on it and stomped down, hard. The phone cracked, practically in half. Pulverized. He did the same to my phone, then to Charlene's camera memory card. "The original documents were burned long ago, in case you were wondering."

"How dare you!" Ms. Hawking shouted from behind us. I turned. She was awake now, but lying on the ground. She hadn't managed to sit up yet.

"Like I've said, some history is best left in the past. Now, it's really been a pleasure speaking with you all, but I have places to be. Besides, I've heard these tunnels are quite unstable and liable to collapse at any time. It really is irresponsible to allow museum patrons to come down here," he said, with a chilling smile. Then he turned and started walking back toward the stairs.

"That isn't true at all," Ms. Hawking shouted down the tunnel after him, instinctively indignant. "I'll have you know they've been inspected by a structural engineer and—"

"Ms. Hawking," I said quietly, and she stopped. I was looking up at the support beams above us. There were little bundles of something rigged up to them, metal boxes connected with wires that spanned beam after beam after beam. In the blink of an eye, all the work lamps went out and left us in complete darkness. And in the silence, there was a very distinct, loud ticking.

THE ESCAPE ROUTE

17

JOE

S SOON AS THE LIGHTS WENT OUT, Ms. Hawking started screaming, her cries echoing down the tunnel.

"Oh no, oh my God, I need to get out of here," she shouted. "Help! Someone help!"

"We have to stay calm," Frank said. "We're going to escape."

I was twisting my arms around as much as I could, trying to reach the front pockets of my shorts, where I'd put my keys and pocketknife. But the bindings were tight and I couldn't get far enough.

"Frank," I said, raising my voice so he could hear me over the curator. "Can you scoot over here and get the keys out of my pocket? The knife is on there."

I could hear Frank shuffling around on the damp planks, and after a few seconds, his shoulder collided with mine.

"Okay, it's in the pocket that's closer to you," I said.

Frank's hands were duct-taped together like mine, but he managed to find the pocket and, eventually, pull the key ring out. I heard the jingling of the keys as he looked for the pocketknife.

"Got it! I've got the pocketknife. Hold on, I'm going to try to cut my hands free," he said.

"Hurry!" the curator wailed.

There was some light grunting in the dark and metallic clinking as Frank worked on the tape. Finally he said, "I've got it! Just a sec, I'm doing my ankles, and then I'll do both of you."

He freed Ms. Hawking next, since she was nearing hysteria. Then he freed my hands and gave me back the knife so I could hack away at the tape around my ankles.

"Does anyone have any kind of flashlight?" Frank asked, not sounding very hopeful.

"Of course no one has a—" Ms. Hawking shouted, but then she paused. "Oh, wait, I have a lighter!" She went into the pocket of her jumpsuit and produced a silver Zippo lighter. The small flame cast a scant amount of light, flickering and inconsistent, but it was something. I finished freeing myself and stood up.

"Can you lift it up so we can see the explosives better?" I said.

Ms. Hawking shuddered. No one had actually called them explosives yet, but that was definitely what we were dealing with. The ticking was continuing from somewhere in the tunnel. Each beam looked to be rigged with three metal devices, each with a small, blinking red light on it. The boxes were connected with multiple wires, which all ran along the wall and down toward the floor.

We followed them a hundred feet or so farther down the tunnel, and there on the floor was a metal box. I leaned over and could hear that the ticking was coming from inside.

"The timer must be in here," I said, looking up at Frank. "Do you think it's safe to open it?"

Frank looked down. "I . . . I don't know. But if we don't open it, we're not going to be able to see if we can turn it off."

I took a deep breath and knelt down next to the box. Slowly, carefully, I opened it up a crack. Nothing happened, except the ticking got louder. I heard Frank let out a sigh of relief.

"I think it's okay," he said. "Let's open it up."

I opened the box the rest of the way, and inside was a timer, counting down from—

"Two minutes," I murmured. "We only have two minutes."

"Well, rip out the wires!" Ms. Hawking said, leaning over my shoulder like she was going to do it herself.

"No, no, wait," I said, putting a hand out to keep her back. "If we take out the wrong one, it could detonate all the bombs. And I have no idea which wire is the right one. Frank . . . do you have any idea?"

He was already shaking his head. "I don't know. I have no clue." There was silence for a moment, besides the ticking.

"Then we have to go," the curator said, with a strange sense of calm, firm authority. "Now."

"But where?" Frank asked.

"Come on," she said, already turning and starting to hurry down the tunnel, away from the entrance to the museum. "Hurry up!"

Frank put out a hand and hauled me up. "Let's go!"

We ran through the tunnel, following the bobbing, flickering light that was Ms. Hawking's lighter. Pretty soon, we caught up with her.

"You said the tunnels go all the way to the East River, right?" I said, forcing the words out. We were all running as hard as we could. I could still hear the ticking behind us.

"Yes," she said, breathless. "They do. I've walked the whole length of them and come out the other side."

"Do you remember how to get there?" I asked.

"I . . . yes, I think so," she replied.

It seemed like we'd only been running for a few seconds when there was a thunderous boom from behind us that sent a shock wave through the whole tunnel. The ground jolted under us and I tripped, crashing into Frank and sending us both onto the ground. Huge chunks of rock, pieces of wood, and clods of dirt were raining down from the ceiling all around.

"Come on, come on!" Ms. Hawking shouted. She grabbed hold of my arm and dragged me to my feet. Frank got back up too and we were all running again as the rumbling and booming and crashing intensified behind us. It sounded like an earthquake. I broke Frank's rule and looked back while running away and saw that the tunnel was rapidly caving in. Dirt and mud and debris like a tidal wave engulfed the space and consumed all traces of air and light. I understood now why Sophie had been so terrified down here. My heart raced.

Eventually, a solid wall came into view in front of us.

"Is that a dead end?" I asked, sneaking another look behind us at the tunnel, which was still collapsing. "Ms. Hawking, is that a dead end?" The second question was forced out as loud as I could with my lungs on fire from running.

"Uh—um," she said, panting.

"Is it?!" Frank shouted.

"No, no, I think it's a fork. We go left and that's how we get to the river." She did not sound very sure. But we really didn't have a lot of options besides following her. Or any other options. To be precise.

We got closer and I could see that she was right. The end of this part of the tunnel split off in two different directions. Ms. Hawking slowed, hesitating for a moment.

"It's left. Yes. I'm sure. Left," she said, seemingly to herself.

Frank and I exchanged a look, but what could we do? We all rounded the corner and ran as hard as we could down the left tunnel for a hundred feet or so.

"Duck and cover!" Frank shouted.

We all stumbled to the ground and covered our heads. Then, with one last thundering crash, the leg of the tunnel we had been in collapsed, covering the way we'd come in rubble and cutting off the entrance to the right part of the tunnel. Mercifully, the cave-in stopped there. But whatever was down this left leg, we were stuck with it now.

Ms. Hawking rested her head against the wall to catch her breath. Frank rolled over, sat up, and rested his head on his knees, doing the same.

"Wow. We made it," I said, half in disbelief. "We're okay."

"As long as this tunnel is actually the one that leads to the river," Frank said.

"Oh ye of little faith," Ms. Hawking said, and lifted up her lighter to illuminate a small enamel sign embedded in the wall opposite where she was sitting. It had squiggly lines on it that looked like running water, with an arrow pointing down the tunnel in the direction we were headed. "It's not too far up ahead now."

LIGHT AT THE END

OF THE TUNNEL

18

FRANK

JOE WHOOPED. "HA! LOOK AT THAT! You did it! We're getting out of here!"

I was so tired and overwhelmed and full of adrenaline, I just started laughing. "Joe, you are completely caked in mud."

He laughed too. "You should see yourself."

Ms. Hawking stood up and wiped a hand across her forehead, smearing the mud that was there as well. "All right, boys, let's get out of here."

She led the way down the tunnel, holding up the flickering lighter in front of her. Gradually, the tunnel seemed to get a little bit brighter.

"Is it just my eyes adjusting, or is there light up ahead?" I asked.

"No, it's light. We're getting closer," Ms. Hawking said.

Soon it was light enough to see without the Zippo, so the curator put it away. Then the end of the tunnel came into view. Just a tiny sparkle of light in the distance at first; then it got bigger and bigger. Soon the brackish, damp smell of the river hit me from up ahead. We finally got to the mouth of the tunnel and stepped out onto the rocky shore, where the East River lapped up against a short, half-rotten dock that connected with the wooden planking on the floor of the tunnel. The sun had fully set now, so we'd been down in the tunnels for . . . it must have been at least an hour. I hoped Charlene was somewhere safe and not too worried sick.

"So this is where Richard Kensington would have escaped to the night of the raid, huh?" Joe asked.

"Indeed, it's likely he came out here. This is the closest tunnel exit to the speakeasy," Ms. Hawking said. "There may have been a rowboat tied up here, or some other secondary escape vehicle." She paused. "I guess we may never know all of what happened, though. Especially now that the documents are gone. And—I don't even want to think about the damage to the museum."

"Well, we have your scans of the documents, plus Charlene's pictures. That's something," I said, hoping it would make her feel at least a little better.

"I suppose so," she said.

"So, um, is there like a ladder up to the street level or something?" Joe asked, looking around.

"Well, people don't usually exit this way. We might have to do a little bit of . . . climbing." Ms. Hawking gave a deep sigh. "Will this day ever end?"

"It'll be over soon," I said, and gave her a tired smile, which she returned.

From out on the edge of the little dock, we could see a rocky embankment that led upward to a metal guardrail.

"I think we might be able to get up this way, if we step in the right places," Joe said. "I'll go first, to test out the footholds."

"Okay," I said. "Just be really careful not to fall in. The river has a current." We were both strong swimmers, but I didn't want any of us to step off the narrow strip of shore and get swept away.

"I will," Joe said. He started up the embankment, wedging one foot between the rocks, then the other, then pulling himself up on solid handholds.

"You should go next, Ms. Hawking. Just grab where he grabs and step where he steps," I said.

She nodded and started climbing up after him. She only slipped once, her foot nearly missing the rock she was trying to step onto, but she recovered her balance quickly and continued on.

I took up the rear, after I saw that Joe was helping Ms. Hawking over the guardrail at the top. I grabbed hold of the lower rocks and stepped off the dock and up. Climbing like this reminded me of hiking and exploring around the lake when my family went on vacation to a rented lake house one summer. Joe and I spent hours climbing on slick rocks and jumping off them into the water. Except right now, I really, really did not want to end up in the water.

I finally made it to the top, and Joe grabbed my wrists and started hauling me up over the guardrail. Once all three of us were up, we stood side by side on the other side of the metal railing.

"Where are we?" Joe finally said.

"We're way down near the bottom of the East River Park. I think if we start walking toward the street, we'll hit Grand," Ms. Hawking said. "I guess we'd better get going."

"We should try to get in touch with the detectives. And with Mr. Lakin and Charlene. We don't want them to think . . ." I thought of the chaos that the huge explosion and cave-in must have caused over at the museum. I wondered if everyone assumed we'd been trapped down there.

"Excuse me!" Joe was walking up to a woman in running clothes who was sitting on a bench, taking a drink from her water bottle. She looked at him and her face changed immediately. We all must have looked awful, caked in mud and debris. "Hi, sorry to bug you. We were just in a bit of an accident. We're okay, but can we possibly borrow your phone for a second?"

"Oh, of course, here you go. Are you sure you're all right?" she said.

"Yeah, just mud. Thanks," Joe said. "I'll try not to let your phone touch my face."

I walked over and stood next to him. "Here, call Charlene." I told him her number, which he dialed and put the call on speaker.

"You've got it memorized?" he said, with a mischievous gleam in his eyes.

"Oh, shush."

The call was picked up after the first ring. "Hello? Hello, who is this?" Charlene sounded stressed.

"Charlene? It's Frank," I said.

"Oh my God, Frank, you're alive! Is Joe there? Did you find Ms. Hawking?" she asked. She sounded so relieved she might cry.

"Yeah, we're all here. Ms. Hawking, too," Joe said.

"Oh man, everyone here is freaking out. The whole museum blew up and caved in! And some of the streets, too, since the tunnels were under them! We weren't sure—the police have a search-and-rescue team coming to look through the tunnels for you all."

"Well, you can tell them we're okay," I said.

"Where are you?" Charlene asked.

"Ms. Hawking said we're at East River Park," Joe said. "Near Grand Street. We got out through the tunnels. All the way to the river."

There was some muffled talking in the background, and then a new voice came through the phone. "Hardys?" It was Detective Smart.

"Yeah, we're here. And so is Ms. Hawking."

The curator was listening over Joe's shoulder.

"Glad you all made it out. It's a serious mess over here. I am going to be buried under an avalanche of paperwork for the rest of—oh, uh, sorry. That was insensitive."

I laughed. "It's okay."

"Listen, can you get to a specific place, like a cross street? I'll send a squad car to pick you up," she said.

"How about Grand and Jackson Street?" Ms. Hawking said.

"Coming right up," Smart replied. "It'll just be a few minutes."

We thanked the jogger and gave back her phone, which looked like it had only a little bit of dirt on it, then followed the curator through the park and out toward the street.

"Did you hear what Charlene said? The tunnel cave-in damaged whole streets up there, since it ran underneath them. Can you believe it?" I asked Joe.

It had been rhetorical, but Ms. Hawking chimed in. Her voice was sort of monotone, gloomy. "Yes, I can believe it. There were miles of tunnels. They ran all over the neighborhood. The cave-ins must have been . . . devastating. The whole museum likely just . . . collapsed into the pit."

After all this, I felt lucky to have exposed the bad guys, to have made it out alive, and to be going home to Bayport tomorrow. But in just a matter of days, Ms. Hawking's life's work had been destroyed. Over what? A power-hungry political type trying to advance his candidate's career. No, let's be honest. His own career.

"I'm so sorry about the museum," I said. "But we know exactly who is responsible. And we have proof. We're going to get them and they're all going to jail for it."

"It isn't going to bring back those documents. Or the artifacts. Or the building," she murmured. And of course, she was right.

We waited on the corner for the squad car, and two young officers picked us up and drove us uptown.

A radius of several blocks around the museum was cordoned off with wooden barriers and squad cars parked sideways across the road. But when we approached, the barricade was moved so we could get through. We parked about a block and a half from the museum and got out. We walked past loads of police cars, accompanied by the officers who had driven us, and as we passed one that had a police officer leaning against the front talking into a walkie-talkie, I stopped in my tracks. Sitting in the back seat, handcuffs on and staring at the headrest in front of him with a vacant expression, was Paul Vander.

"Joe!" I said, taking his shoulder and turning him toward it.

"Oh, yeah," one of the officers with us said. "We caught that one red-handed leaving the museum just before the explosion. Let me tell you, attempted triple murder by way of nearly blowing up a city block is no joke. That guy is going away for a long, long time."

"Good," Ms. Hawking said from behind us. "As he should."

The officers took us to a huge white-and-blue van that looked a bit like a fire truck. It said NYPD MOBILE COMMAND CENTER on the side.

"We're not getting any closer to the museum," one of them explained. "The sidewalk is unstable." She went up and knocked on the door, and it was opened by Detective Santos, who ushered us in. Sitting inside were Charlene and Mr. Lakin, along with Detective Smart and loads of other police officers, who were busily pushing past one another in the narrow space to go about their work, like bees in a hive.

"You're here!" Charlene said, and jumped up from her seat. She came over and wrapped Joe and me in a hug. "I'm so glad you're okay."

"I'm glad you're okay too. Did you get out before the explosion in the tunnels?" I asked.

"Yeah, I did. I was about to call the detectives anyway, because it had been so long, but as soon as I got that weird text message from your phone, I knew something was really wrong. You'd never use numbers for abbreviations like that."

Joe gave me a devilish look, and I knew he would rag on

me later about how much the two of us must text for her to know my patterns so well.

Charlene continued, "So I called them right away and told them everything, and that you must have been captured too. I got out of the store and was watching from across the street when Vander and those goons came booking it out of there. Luckily, the detectives were just pulling up and surrounded all of them. And that was when the explosions happened. It was like an earthquake! I thought . . ." She looked down at her hands, clenched in front of her. "Well, I mean, we all thought you might be trapped down there. How did you get out?"

We told everyone what had happened in the tunnels and everything Vander had confessed in his classic villain speech.

"I almost forgot about the article!" I said. It had just hit me out of nowhere. "Charlene, did it auto-send?"

"No, it didn't auto-send," she said. "I pressed send on it myself. People have a right to know, with an election on the line. That's a journalist's job. But more than that, Nicky Facchini deserves to have his family's name cleared."

"Oh, man, Nicky!" I said. In all of this, I'd forgotten about him. I turned to Detective Smart. "We saw the warrant on your desk. Did you actually arrest him for the break-ins? Have you cleared him of everything now?"

She and her partner exchanged a look. "*Unbelievable* that you were snooping on my desk," she said, shaking her head. "I was prepping the warrant, but it wasn't signed yet.

Obviously, in light of everything, he's free of all suspicion with our sincere apologies."

"Well, that's a relief," Joe said. "Although, if the museum caved in, so did his store. That's awful. I hope he has insurance."

"He does," Ms. Hawking said quietly. "A while back the building had a leak and we talked about submitting our claims."

"Well, at least there's that," Charlene said, with a sigh.

"I just don't understand how people honestly think they can get away with these things," Detective Smart said, shaking her head. "It blows my mind. Well, you kids almost got yourselves killed and you absolutely should not have gone about it this way. But I've got to hand it to you. You did figure it out."

Detective Santos turned to Mr. Lakin. "You all are leaving on the morning Amtrak?" It was almost a question, but not really.

"Yes, definitely," he said, sounding shaken. "I still don't know what I am going to tell these kids' parents."

"They're kind of used to it at this point, Mr. Lakin," Joe observed.

"All right, well, let's get you all back to the hotel. Thank you, officers, for everything," he said.

We all thanked Santos and Smart and said our goodbyes to Ms. Hawking, wishing her all the best in rebuilding the museum. If anyone could do it, I thought, it would be her.

When we got back to the hotel, Joe and I had to flip a coin for who got to take a shower first. Joe won, but thankfully he was quick and I was able to wash all the rubble and grime off and change clothes without waiting too long. Just as we were settling in for an evening *Law & Order* marathon to wind down after one of the more stressful days in recent memory, there was a knock on the door.

Joe and I looked at each other. "Uh, all those Vander goons got arrested, right?" Joe asked.

I went to the door and looked through the peephole, then broke into a huge smile. I opened it on Charlene, holding a pizza box.

"One large New York pizza for Joe Hardy," she said. "And Frank, too. And I'm definitely having a slice. Can I come in?"

"Absolutely," I said, stepping aside.

"Oh, no way! Awesome!" Joe exclaimed, jumping off the bed and running over. "It smells amazing."

"Yeah, as soon as we got back here, I realized I was starving. That rescue mission was right in the middle of dinnertime," she said.

Joe was already digging into the pizza. "Oh my God, it's so good," he said. "Frank, have some of this."

I grabbed a slice and a paper plate from the stack that Charlene brought. She'd thought of everything. Then I held it up toward Joe and Charlene. "Cheers to another successful case!"

Joe and Charlene lifted their pizza slices too, laughing.

"You're going to have to join us on cases more often, Charlene. You're a pretty great detective," I said.

She smiled. "Anytime."

New mystery. New suspense. New danger.

Nancy Drew DIARIES™

BY CAROLYN KEENE

NANCYDREW.COM

EBOOK EDITIONS ALSO AVAILABLE

Aladdin | simonandschuster.com/kids

Middle school is hard.

Solving cases for the FBI is even harder. Doing both at the same time—well, that's just crazy. But that doesn't stop Florian Bates! Get to know the only kid who hangs out with FBI agents *and* international criminals.

Looking for another great book?
Find it
IN THE MIDDLE.

Fun, fantastic books for kids
in the in-be**TWEEN** age.

IntheMiddleBooks.com

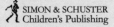

READ & LEARN

with
simon kids

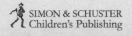
75458